GLACIER'S THAW

POSEIDON'S WARRIORS
BOOK 10

DARLENE TALLMAN

INTERNATIONAL BESTSELLING AUTHOR
DARLENE TALLMAN

COPYRIGHT

This is a work of fiction. Names, characters, places, and incidents are either the product of the author's imagination or used fictitiously, and any resemblance to actual persons, living or dead, business establishments, events or locales is entirely coincidental.

Glacier's Thaw - A Poseidon's Warriors MC novel
Initial story featured in "Rescued" TNTNYC anthology released
10/7/23
Copyright 2023© Darlene Tallman
Published by: Darlene Tallman

ALL RIGHTS RESERVED. This book contains material protected under International and Federal Copyright Laws and Treaties. Any unauthorized reprint or use of this material is prohibited. No part of this book may be reproduced or transmitted in any form or by any means, electronic or mechanical, including photocopying, recording, or by any information storage and retrieval system without express written permission from. Darlene Tallman, the author / publisher.

Cover Model: Landon Lee
Photographer: FuriousFotog/Golden Czermak
Editors: Nicole McVey, Beth DiLoreto, Sylvie Howick
Proofers: Nicole Lloyd, Nicole McVey, Cheryl Hullett
Formatter: Liberty Parker
Cover by Tracie Douglas of Dark Water Covers

The Devil's Riot MC characters are copyrighted and written by E.C. Land and used with permission for this particular story, as well as the extended version. A list of her characters is provided.

PWMC CAST OF CHARACTERS

Jesse "Poseidon" Malone - President (Lilli; daughter - Winnie; daughter - Melody)
Callum "Loki" O'Rourke - Vice President (CeeCee; daughter - Hayden)
Brock "Trident" Storm - Enforcer (Gianna; daughter - Finley aka Finnie; daughter - Collette; daughter - Alexia)
Gannon Brooks - Sergeant-at-Arms (Hayley; son - Micah; daughter - Mariah)
Ky "Orion" Stanford - Treasurer (Roane; daughter - Rosie; daughter - Roxie)
Beck "Atlas" Crandall - Secretary (Patsy; daughter - Talia)
Tyson "Specks" Leone - IT (Kaya; son - Noah; daughter - Peyton)
Canyon Masters - Patched member - (Chelsea Grant)
Asa "Glacier" Smith - newly Patched member

Nate "Shark" Atkins - newly Patched member

Club Businesses

Tattoo Parlor

Bike/Automotive Repair Shop/Custom Helmets

Security/PI business

Additional Characters

Koba - Atlas' service dog

Ridley - Patsy's service dog

Smokey/Smokey Joe - Chelsea's service dog

Tessie

Momma M (CeeCee's foster mom/Patsy's mom)

Mary & Shamus O'Reilly (Hayley's family of choice)

Granny (Kaya's grandmother)

DEVIL'S RIOT MC SOUTHEAST MEMBERS

WRITTEN BY E.C. LAND

O – Ol' Lady, C – Child
Hammer – Prez – Avery – O
Tate – C
Malice – VP – Willow – O
Gates – C
Gavin – C
Gemini – C
Axe – Sergeant at Arms – CJ – O
Savage – Road Captain – Honor – O
Gunner – Enforcer – Zinnia – O
Delilah – C
Cy – Tech
Bruiser – Treasurer
Dagger – Medic
Rogue – Secretary – Rebel – O
Brass – Chaplain

Glock – Member
Ruger – Member
Blade – Member
Colt – Member
Carbine – Member

ACKNOWLEDGMENTS

Thanks to Janine Infante Bosco for once again creating two anthologies so that another of my PWMC guys could get "his" story told! I can't wait for everyone to read this expanded version; the anthology was literally just a taste of things to come.

Also, thanks to my collab partner, E.C. Land, for writing "Savage's Honor" the other piece to this particular puzzle. I had a great time zipping up to Virginia so we could work in person, and can't wait until we reveal the other things up our proverbial sleeves!

Darlene

DEDICATION

For my AliG and SweetTart. Y'all aren't old enough to read my books yet, but I wanted to do this because the weekend I came up to Virginia to work with E.C., I was able to do dinner with you guys, as well as my favorite oldest son and beautiful, favorite oldest daughter-in-love. Always remember, I love y'all to the moon and back again.

Love,

Grandma Darlene

AUTHOR'S NOTE

This book, Glacier's Thaw, deals with some hard subjects, including sexual assault, physical abuse, and suicide. While every effort was made not to glamorize any of these things, and some details were left more to the reader's imagination, there may be scenes that are traumatic and/or triggering. This wasn't my intent; I was trying to convey the sheer terror Delaney felt upon her discovery and based on feedback, I was able to do so. However, if any of the above topics are triggering, please don't read this book as that's something I don't want to happen to any of my readers!

Also, you'll see comparable scenes in E.C. Land's book, "Savage's Honor." This was intentional; you need to see them from multiple points of view, and we rewrote them in our books as needed with that in mind. Some of hers are glossed over while I go into more detail and vice versa, so you're able to read them both in whatever order you prefer!

Darlene

BLURB

Glacier

I'm awkward, socially inept, and if it wasn't for the men in my club who I now call brother, I'm unsure if I'd still be kicking around this ol' earth. Life isn't kind to those who face challenges, especially when they're not physically visible. Still, I'm not without blood family, so when I find out my cousin's club, the Devil's Riot MC, has placed an order for custom helmets, I offer to make the delivery. That way, I can see my cousin, Honor, as well, and meet her roommate. I never expected to leave for my trip as soon as I did, nor did I expect it to be because Honor's been taken.

Only, after meeting Delaney and being totally captivated by her, I have to wonder, who's rescuing whom?

Delaney

When I realize my roommate is facing an imminent medical crisis, I head to her workplace to see what's going on. I never expected to hear that she didn't show up, or to find her car with evidence to suggest she was taken. Countless calls to her brother go unanswered, so I try the next person on her ICE list, her cousin.

Meeting Asa, or Glacier as his patch on his leather vest denotes, sends sparks of awareness through me, but Honor is more important right now. I can always explore how I'm feeling later, right?

Two different clubs come together to find one beloved family member; the question remains - who's the damaged party and who's being rescued?

Suitable for ages 18+ due to adult content, situations, and language

PROLOGUE

Asa, age 5

"You're a stupid little creep," my father seethed from his position over me, while I laid on the floor, my eye already swelling shut. I can taste the blood on my lip but manage to hold back my tears.

He doesn't like it when I cry. Says it means I'm a 'pussy' and even though I don't understand what he's telling me, I know it's not nice. I don't answer him, unsure of what I did to cause him to backhand me, but I know he'll tell me. He always does.

"Wasted my time today, boy," he growled, the tip of his boot striking my side. "How hard is it for you to fucking act normal? Now your fucking teacher wants you to be tested because she thinks you're 'on the spectrum' whatever the fuck *that* means."

The pain now radiating from the continued blows has me biting back my whimper. The angrier he gets, the more he loses control. I just wish I understood what he was talking about; I liked school. The schedule, the order of tasks; all of it helped soothe something inside of me. I mean, I know I tended to focus on some things more than others, but my teacher, Miss Hatcher, was always kind.

"Straighten up and fly right, Asa, or you'll regret it," he warned, storming out of my bedroom.

Leaving me broken and bleeding on my floor once again. It takes me a long time before I'm able to pick myself up, and even longer to go to the bathroom so I can clean up my face. I'm already thinking of what excuse I can give the next time I have school for the bruise that covers the right side. I don't think Miss Hatcher believes me, but I'll stick to my story and hopefully, she won't push for more.

Because my body can't take too much more of my father's 'love' and 'correction'.

Asa, age 6

We moved again so I'm at a new school. I don't like this one as much; the other kids pick on me a lot, shoving me down then laughing when I end up hurt. Between my father and the bullies, I'm constantly covered in bruises. Right now, I've got a cast on my left arm, a product of 'falling' down the stairs, although in reality, my father pushed me because I wasn't moving fast enough to suit him. It's hard for me to move sometimes when my sides hurt. Sometimes, I wish I had never been born; I'm a waste of space apparently.

While the other kids talked to each other, I sat at my desk and drew in my notebook. I'm so focused on shading in an area that I didn't notice when the room went silent until I heard my teacher, Mrs. Smith, say, "Asa, please gather your belongings and go to the office with Mr. Hall."

As the kids all started whispering that I must be in trouble, I shoved my stuff into my backpack then stood. Somehow, I knew that I wouldn't be back, which was both a good thing and a bad thing.

Mr. Hall, our principal, smiled kindly at me while holding out his arm for me to follow him. "It's going to be okay, Asa. I promise," he said.

Walking into his office, I saw a lady and two police

officers. Sitting down, I waited for them to tell me what was going on, my fingers tapping against my jeans-clad leg. Another of my 'quirks' that made my dad so angry; I couldn't stop fidgeting whenever I was sitting down.

"Asa, we're here because there was an accident involving your father," one of the police officers stated. "Unfortunately, he died, and because he was your sole parent, you'll be going into foster care."

I'm stunned. Here I was wishing I was dead and instead, my father died. I'm unsure how to feel; I know he never loved me. I was just a worthless piece of shit.

"What about my stuff?" I asked.

I didn't have a lot of things, but I didn't want to lose anything either. I had a few treasured books, my sketch pads, and my pencils. Because even though my father didn't concern himself about 'inconsequential events' like my birthday or Christmas, the neighbor lady always gave me something to celebrate the occasion. She did it in secret though, when my dad was out of the house because he would've thrown them away. I keep them hidden, only pulling them out when he's out to the bar or at work.

Yes, I stay home by myself. The neighbor lady watches the house and whenever she saw my dad leave, she'd bring me a plate of food. Sometimes, she got me clothes. They were hand-me-downs from her own children, but at least they were clean and not torn up. He never noticed, but it helped me feel a little more like everyone else.

"We'll go by your house and gather your belongings," the woman who had been sitting silently stated.

She lied.

I never saw my old house again and went into my foster home with the clothes on my back and what was in my backpack.

Asa, age 9

Another foster home, another school. I'm still kind of small for my age, but I've learned how to fight back. I won't start anything, but I definitely don't allow anyone to beat on me any longer. I guess I can thank the second home I was in because the foster dad was worse than my own father, and he was awful.

My teachers don't know how to deal with a kid like me. My father never got any testing done, saying it was a waste of time, so they do the best they can, and I struggle to learn basic concepts. Hearing dummy, stupid, and even worse, the 'r' word makes me wonder why I'm still alive.

But every time I think maybe I should just give up and figure out a way out of this miserable existence, something deep inside tells me to keep holding on.

For what, I have no clue.

Asa, age 12

"I'm Honor, who are you?" the girl asked, standing in front of me.

"I'm Asa," I replied.

I was in *another* foster home, but this one seemed different. I was still holding back because I had been burned so many times over the past six years, all the hope I held had dwindled down to a small ember that was in danger of going out.

"You'll like it here," she promised as I unpacked my suitcase in the dresser that Mrs. Johnson told me was mine to use.

"I guess we'll see," I replied.

"I've been here a few years, you'll see what I mean. Hurry up and unpack, I want to show you the treehouse in the backyard."

Shrugging at her enthusiasm, I finished my task, put the empty suitcase in the closet, then followed her downstairs and outside. That first day, we spent hours in the treehouse, comparing stories about being in the system. Her older brother wasn't able to get custody of her because of his age, so she hadn't seen him in a long time. She told me she had ADHD when she saw me fidgeting.

"I don't think that's what's wrong with me," I admitted. "A long time ago, my father said one of my teachers told him she thought I was on the spectrum. I still don't know what that means, though."

"Let's go ask!" she exclaimed, climbing out of the treehouse. "Mr. Johnson is very smart, he can help us figure it out."

I was skeptical, but followed her anyway, glad that someone wanted to be around me for a change.

Asa, age 13

"Honor, Asa, come here!" Mr. Johnson yelled. "The results came back and you're not going to believe what they said."

We abandoned our homework and ran to where he was standing, smiling from ear to ear. "What did it say?" Honor asked, while I stood back.

A few months ago, Mr. Johnson started doing some genealogy stuff and when Honor mentioned having a brother, he swabbed both of us and submitted it to some site to see if either of us had any other family out there.

"Well, the two of you are cousins for starters," Mr. Johnson announced. At our stunned looks, he continued. "It seems that someone in your family started a chart, and the relationship is on your mother's side, Honor. Asa, you're no longer all alone in this world."

A small smile crossed my face. Honor had become my best friend, helping me navigate the perils of middle school while making sure I understood what I was being taught. The Johnsons asked my caseworker about testing, but she pushed it off, so they researched everything they could find about autism, and started implementing small things that made a big difference in how I coped every day.

For the first time in my life, I was kind of fitting in. I was still cautious when it came to opening up to other people, but I had a few friends.

"We're cousins, we're cousins," Honor sang, giggling and grabbing my arm. "We'll always be close, too, right?" she asked.

"Absolutely," I promised.

Asa, age 19

"I promise, Honor, I'll be careful," I said as I grabbed my

duffel bag. "I've got your number and I'll keep in touch."

"Don't you dare ghost me, Asa, I'll be pissed if you do," she retorted.

Since we aged out of the system, I brought her up to where her brother, Gunner lived. He was in a motorcycle club, something that intrigued me. I saw how his brothers were; they watched out for each other, and when they found out Honor was his sister, they became super protective.

The best thing though, was Gunner taught me how to ride. I didn't have the money to buy my own bike yet, so I was shocked when he offered his old bike to me. We spent hours working on it to get it road worthy again, then he and several of his brothers rode with me to make sure I knew what I was doing. Gotta admit, aside from when we lived with the Johnsons, his club is the closest thing I've ever had to a family environment. I just knew I needed to get away, make my own path in life. I found I had an affinity for painting, so maybe I'll find somewhere I can perfect my craft.

Chuckling, I pulled her in for a one-armed hug then turned and walked away. It was time to see if I could make it in this cruel world. The good thing was, I was as cold as ice thanks to all the shit I'd had shoveled at me.

And the only woman I'd ever love would be my cousin, Honor.

Because women couldn't be trusted. Bethany Jayne Northrup proved that to me two years ago and any heart I might've had was encased in a block of impenetrable ice. I'd fuck 'em and go; no strings, no emotions, no hurt ever again.

I hated that she was crying; we'd spent so many hours together over the past several years, sharing our hopes and dreams, but even though I loved hanging around with Gunner and his brothers, their club was not for me.

"Suck it up, buttercup," Gunner yelled. "It's not like he's dropping off the face of the fucking earth. As for you," he says, pointing at me, "dress for the ride and slide, not to look good. You got me?"

"Yeah, I got you, cuz," I replied. One of his other brothers had outgrown his leathers and passed them on to me, so other than the parts I bought for my bike, and a helmet that had Bluetooth capability, I hadn't spent all that much.

I'd still be able to eat, at least until I found somewhere to land and could get a job.

CHAPTER ONE

Delaney

"I'm glad your brother and his friends were able to help us move into our apartment," I say, looking over at Honor as she unpacks a box marked 'kitchen'.

"Right? Of course, you *know* he had Cy do a background check on you," she replies, grinning at me.

"Wouldn't expect anything less," I retort.

The first time Honor and I met was in college at the campus bookstore. We were both looking for the same book because we had the same class. We ended up talking the whole time we got the rest of our stuff, then we went to the campus cafe.

From that moment on, we've been best friends, which has us now in our own apartment after slogging through the hell that was college. She's a nurse at the local hospital; I'm a special education teacher for the county school system. Basically, the kids I have are bussed from all over the county to a centralized location so I can teach them.

It's not easy. Some days, I come home exhausted and cry, wondering if I'll ever make a difference in one of their lives. Other days? Seeing one of 'my' kids have what I refer to as a lightbulb moment reminds me that small steps yield great rewards.

Thankfully, I have three aides who help with some of the kids who need a little more hands-on care; otherwise, I wouldn't be able to do it.

"He's just… overprotective," she says.

"Honor, I get it and totally understand. Now, I know all we have to do is unpack our stuff for our rooms and the little bit of kitchen stuff thanks to the old ladies who came to help, but I want some chips and queso plus a few frozen margaritas to celebrate us being adults."

"It's ol' lady."

"That's what I said," I reply.

"No, you said *old*, and it's actually ol'."

GLACIER'S THAW

"Fine, fine, I'm not hip on biker lingo you know," I tease.

"Stick with me and I'm sure you'll pick it up in no time. Now, I vote for going and picking up what we want since Avery and Willow brought us a blender, so we can drink as much as we want in the comfort of our own home."

"Let me grab my keys."

"This might not have been the best idea," I mumble as I crawl out of my bed, my eyes squinted nearly shut from the incessant light coming through the blinds I forgot to close last night. "That last pitcher was a bad idea."

Thank God it's the weekend. As I shuffle into my bathroom, I turn the shower on to heat the water then strip out of yesterday's clothes. Yeah, we were wrecked by the time we finally crashed, so my makeup is all gunked up on my face and I feel as though I smell like a goat.

Once I'm sure the water's at the toasty level of hell I prefer, I step inside and let out a groan of relief as it sluices over my shoulders and down my back. Despite the muscle we had from Honor's brother and his friends, we still did our fair share of lifting, and my body is aching all over.

Grabbing my shampoo, I quickly lather up then rinse, before doing it again. After rinsing the second time, I put my conditioner in then go about washing my body and shaving my legs and pits. I might be single, but I was raised to always be presentable from the skin out.

Memories fly through my brain as I finally get all the conditioner out of my hair and then take the hand-held shower head to make sure there's no soap residue left on my body.

"Delaney, a proper young lady doesn't go out without makeup."

"Delaney, stand up straight, don't slouch. Posture is important."

"Delaney, I don't understand your obsession with those clothes. They're totally inappropriate for a young woman of your position."

"Position," I sneer, grabbing a towel for my hair and winding it around like a turban before I slip on my terrycloth robe. The only 'position' we had growing up was one that was all in my mother's head. Still, I suffered through and endured years of her teachings about what a proper young lady should look like, say, wear, and do. Now that I'm on my own, disowned because I took a stand concerning one of my cousins, I do what I want.

Thanks to Honor. She thinks I saved her, but the opposite is true. I was so uptight when we first met, it's truly a miracle that she broke through my reserve and became my friend. As I lotion my body, one of the habits I can't break, but since it keeps my skin smooth, I don't worry too much, I think about my cousin, Ada.

She was born with several disabilities that left her confined to a wheelchair. While the doctors felt she would never be able to learn because she was nearly non-verbal, my aunt and uncle found the best therapists and medical professionals they could, and they worked with her constantly. Since she was only two years younger than me, I was fascinated by the techniques her aides used, and was often by their side helping.

Ada's the primary reason I became a special education teacher. While she's never going to be able to live on her own, instead of being dumped in an assisted living facility, she's in a group home with other young adults like her. They've got several 'house parents' who live on site, who provide the helping hands for each of the residents that they need according to their abilities. Seeing her face when she accomplishes a task that most of us would take for granted has been my driving force behind every technique I use in my classroom, as well as the information I gather for each parent so they can work with their kids at home.

Only... my parents *hated* my passion with a well,

passion. Several times I was threatened by them of losing my money for school, so I made sure I got scholarships to cover my tuition and books, and found a part-time job working for one of the services that provides care to the place Ada lives. When my aunt and uncle found out what my parents were doing, they also chipped in so when I finally graduated, I was without student debt.

Shaking my head to rid it of the gloomy thoughts my parents evoke, I hang my robe up and stroll through my bedroom to the closet, naked except for the towel on my head. Since I suspect we'll mostly be puttering around the apartment getting things fully settled, I opt for a pair of sweats and an old t-shirt, forgoing a regular bra for my sports bra.

"Bras should be outlawed," I grumble as I maneuver myself into the one-piece lycra bra. "They're torture devices, even these things."

"Totally agree," Honor replies, walking into my room. "Hey, can I French braid your hair today? It should hold for a day or two and you'll have some wicked waves on Monday at school."

"Sure, why not?"

"Something's not right, she's usually waiting in the living room with bated breath when I go out on a date," I whisper as I close and lock the door behind me. We've been in our apartment for six months now and are settled in as well as we're gonna get.

The living room is dark; the only light coming from the one over the stove which we leave on all the time. Hanging up my keys on the hook by the door, I slide my shoes off, grateful to ditch the heels, place my purse on the side table and head into the bathroom to take care of my overfull bladder.

My date was such a blowhard, I'm surprised I didn't come up with an excuse to leave. The whole time we were together, he did nothing but talk about himself. His achievements, his financial status, his aspirations for the future.

"Who are you kidding?" I state out loud as my pantyhose are practically ripped off and tossed into the hamper. "You tried calling Honor when you were in the bathroom, remember?" I giggle as I sit there letting nature take its course. Finally finished, I flush then wash my hands, looking at my reflection in the mirror. "Only, she didn't answer. Then, you texted her and it still shows as 'delivered' which is even stranger."

Heading out of the bathroom toward Honor's bedroom, I call out, "Honor? Did you fall asleep, woman? You're supposed to be my backup if shit goes south." Opening up her door, I see her curled up on the bed, but she doesn't look right. Rushing to her side, I touch her and see she's clammy, but she's breathing. She's been complaining about headaches lately, and can't seem to quench her thirst, but since she's a nurse and told me there was nothing to worry about, I didn't press.

This time, however, she doesn't get a choice as I'm unable to rouse her, either by calling her name or shaking her. So, I call 911.

"No, no, no! You can't tell Gunner, he'll put me under lock and key," Honor protests from her hospital bed.

"You could've *died*, Honor," I retort. "The doctor said it's a good thing I found you because you were practically in a diabetic coma. Why did you ignore all the warning signs?" I ask.

"Because I'm an adult and they don't develop Type 1 diabetes," she replies, sticking her tongue out at me.

"Apparently, they do," I mutter, looking at my best friend. As soon as I told the paramedics some of what she had recently been complaining of, I saw a lightbulb go off over their heads and as they hooked up IVs, one was calling in to the hospital to advise of the possible situation, while the other pricked her finger with a lancet and tested her blood sugar.

Personally, I may not know a lot about this disease, but even I knew that her result of four hundred was entirely too high. Which is why I'm now trying to convince her to let me call her brother. He needs to know; hell, everyone she knows should be aware of her medical condition just in case she has something like this happen again while she's learning how to regulate things.

"Please, Delaney. I know you don't know him all that well, but I'm telling you, he's an alpha male to the core. This isn't something he can 'fix', so he'll want to be in my business twenty-four/seven, and I won't be able to breathe!" she exclaims.

She makes a valid point. Gunner is intense. Hell, all the brothers in his club are that way; they're quite intimidating, which is why I've only accompanied Honor once or twice to the clubhouse when they were having family days. All that scrutiny makes me want to confess to the piece of bubble gum I took from the candy jar when I was five. Or how I chose to use Cliff Notes for some of my English Lit reports. I kind of felt bad; but I *did* skim the books, I just couldn't handle reading them all the way through! They may be considered to be some of the best written books of the nineteenth century, but I classified them as boring. While I've fallen asleep reading before, it's usually when I choose to read before bed.

With those books, I was dozing off within the first few paragraphs. Regardless, I got good grades on them and in the end, that was all that mattered to me.

"Then, if you don't want me telling him, we're going to have a system of sorts so I can keep an eye on things as well. I presume you don't plan to tell your coworkers either?" I ask. I don't like keeping something like this from her brother; I feel like it's going to come back and bite us both in the ass at some point, but right now, I'll go along with it.

"Nope. Once we go through the classes the doctor mentioned, it should be easy peasy to stay straight and fly right," she says, grinning at me.

"I'm not kidding, Honor," I warn. "I never want to come home to see you like that again. It was terrifying." My mind replays how I find her, and my tears start flowing again. "I thought you were either dead or actually dying. You can't do that shit to me, do you hear?"

"Fine, fine. I'm sure there's an app or something that will allow you to know what's going on," she sing-songs.

"And if Gunner ever finds out, I'm throwing you under the bus. I don't want to find myself taking a ride to the local pig farm or something."

"You watch too many shows. Gunner's club is nothing like that," she teases. At my relieved breath, she continues. "They've got a vat of lye out back."

Now horrified, I stare at her, my mouth gaping open like a fish out of water until she bursts into laughter. "Oh my God, you should see your face!" She continues cackling while I work to restore my heart rate to a normal level.

"You're such a bitch," I grumble.

"Yeah, but I'm *your* bitch," she returns.

CHAPTER TWO

Delaney

For the past six months, I've watched the app like a hawk, but other than the occasional spikes, Honor's done really well keeping her blood sugar levels in the range the doctor recommended. Thankfully, she's regained the weight she lost before she was diagnosed; she was starting to look gaunt which is something I know Gunner would have eventually noticed. I'm still not sure how she pulled off any questions when she did see him, because as obvious as it was to me and I see her every day, it was likely more noticeable to anyone who hasn't seen her in a few weeks.

Right now, I'm on my own as her cousin, Asa, came to visit. Unfortunately, I have a conference for work, so I'm out of town. She's been wanting us to meet for a long time, but it hasn't happened, which is disappointing because I actually *want* to meet him.

While she says he doesn't do relationships, she's showed me pictures of him, and I find my heart racing whenever thoughts of him pop into my head. He's not a huge guy, which I think would intimidate me tremendously, but he's well-muscled and has that scruff on his face that makes me think dark and delicious thoughts.

Sighing, I grab the remote in my hotel room and see what I can find to watch. In a lot of ways, because of how I was raised, I'm such a homebody. While the rest of the people I am with are downstairs partying it up at the bar, I've already showered after today's session and am in my comfy onesie. Giggling, I look down at it, seeing the flying pigs, complete with sparkles. Honor found it and since I tend to say 'when pigs fly' she couldn't resist picking it up for me. It's one of my favorite pairs of pajamas, as evidenced by the slight hole in the knee. I ordered some food and snacks from an app, and once they were delivered, I've been holed up ever since.

"Oh wow, it's a *Cold Case* marathon," I mumble. "Gotta watch it for sure."

Satisfied with my viewing choice, I finish eating my Chinese food then get up and toss the trash before grabbing the snacks I think I'll want for the night, along with my phone. Checking my texts, I see one from Honor and open it, only to burst out laughing at the picture she sent.

It's a selfie of her and Asa and he doesn't look happy that she's taking the picture, while she's mugging it up.

Me: Oh my God, Honor! He looks like he wants to kill you!

Honor: He hates getting his picture taken. Always has, ever since we were kids. But I told him we needed to commemorate his trip.

Me: Monitor looks good.

Honor: Yes, mother I'm behaving myself.

Me: Don't start, hussy.

Honor: I promise I'm behaving, D. The doctor is happy with my progress, and I'm doing the food log thingie the nutritionist recommended.

Me: How was work? I feel like I've been gone forever since we didn't see each other before I left!

Honor: I know! It was work, to be honest. They floated me up to the surgical floor, which was different.

Me: How so?

Honor: Well, most of the patients were still groggy from surgery, or due for pain meds. Made it kind of easy.

Me: So, you didn't spend an hour or so after your shift was over doing all your charting?

Honor: Exactly! I mean, most of them are done on time, of course, but I usually don't have time to do all my observations which is frustrating as hell!

Me: I'm not interrupting your time with Asa, am I?

Honor: LOL. No, he and Gunner went for a ride. I guess my brother did some kind of modification on his bike and he wanted to check it out.

Me: Boys and their toys, huh?

Honor: Right? What are you up to? How was the seminar today?

Me: Sitting here watching a Cold Case marathon. Just ate some dinner. The seminar was okay, I guess. A lot of the participants have never heard of some of the newer techniques being used to help the kids learn. So, there were a lot of questions.

Honor: At least the school system lets you have input on the curriculum you use.

Me: Very true. Each of the kids has had a baseline test, but I'm already seeing measurable improvements with several of them. Can't tell you what that means to me.

Honor: I wish we'd have had a teacher like you growing up.

Me: What do you mean?

Honor: Um, well, it's not my story to tell, but Asa struggled in several areas, and of course, my ADHD had me bouncing off the damn walls half the time. It's a miracle we graduated. It's not that either of us are stupid or anything, we just don't learn the same way as most people.

Me: No one is 'stupid', Honor! Some peoples' brains are just wired differently and it's up to the teacher to figure out the best way to get them to understand what they're being taught.

> Honor: Well, I'm gonna run, D. Got my lunch packed for tomorrow already, but I need to make sure my scrubs look good. Apparently, the big wigs plan to come around and despite the fact I'm usually in the ER where chaos reigns, I have to look all bright and shiny according to my supervisors.

> Me: So, what do y'all do if you've had a trauma and have blood everywhere?

> Honor: Well… it's why I'm packing extra clothes because normally, we just grab something else and change, but it might not match what we're already wearing, y'know? Only tomorrow, we gotta match.

> Me: Sounds like bullshit to me.

> Honor: Same. Talk to you tomorrow!

> Me: Behave! Love your guts.

> Honor: Love your liver!

I wake up disoriented and realize I must've dozed off. Sitting up, I see my marathon is still playing, so I leave it on, set the sleep timer on the television, then get up and throw out all the trash from my junk food feast.

"May as well pee while I'm up," I grumble, stumbling toward the bathroom. I seem to remember my grandmother saying that a lot when she got older which in my tired state, has me giggling.

Once I've done my business, I brush my teeth, recheck the door to make sure it's still locked, then glance at my outfit for the next day to make sure I'm as prepared as possible. I went over the topics in the binder we were given and jotted some notes down as well as some questions, which I hope we get to.

As I crawl back between the sheets, my mind is swirling with how many ways there are now to teach someone basic skills. Several decades ago, there wasn't much hope for a child who was on the spectrum, or even one who was profoundly disabled, but nowadays, there are techniques and ways to ensure they're able to learn something.

A tear slips out when I think of one of my students from last year, Joshua. There was a birth injury that deprived him of oxygen which caused him to develop cerebral palsy. He was one of the sweetest little boys I ever met, only six, but despite his struggle with delayed motor skill development, as well as difficulty speaking, he never stopped trying. Every day, he'd come to class and while he struggled, he worked hard and when he'd master something, his smile was so radiant, it lit up the room.

Sadly, while on Christmas break, his family's house caught fire, and he and his father succumbed to the injuries they sustained while his dad was trying to get him out of the house. However, his determination despite his obvious physical limitations, is what continues to drive me.

"You're still so missed, little man," I whisper as sleep claims me. "You'll never be forgotten."

CHAPTER THREE

Glacier

"Listen, brat, the sooner I'm off the phone, the sooner I'm headed in your direction," I state, grinning as I toss clothes into my duffel bag.

"I know, I know, but I was going to see if you'd maybe stop at Buc-ee's and get me some more of the saltwater taffy I like. Pretty please?" Honor asks, making me chuckle out loud.

"I'll see if I have any room in my saddlebags," I tease, quickly making my bed.

"There's always room for taffy," she retorts.

"Fine, fine. What flavor again?"

"*Asa*," she grumbles. "You should know by now there's

only one acceptable flavor, although Delaney thinks there's a second one as well."

My ears perk up at the mention of her roommate. "What's that?" I ask.

"Well, peppermint is the cool flavor, but if you like living on the fringes of life, you might enjoy cinnamon as well," she replies, giggling. "Don't tell her I told you this, but I kinda like the cinnamon too, I just like to give her shit about her choice."

"And am I taking you two to dinner finally?" I question. It seems that every time I've gone up to visit, her roommate has been out of town for one thing or another. She's apparently a special education teacher, and goes to a lot of conferences to learn new shit or something.

"Well… you can take me," she sing-songs. "But D is at a workshop again. I think the universe is conspiring against me being able to introduce the two of you!"

"It's all good, Honor. Not like I'm looking for a woman in my life."

No, I'll just do what I've been doing; go into town, hit up the bar and find a one-nighter when my hand gets too old.

"Asa, I think you'd really like her, though. She's super smart, but she doesn't shove it in your face, you know what I mean?"

"Yeah, brat, I hear ya. So that means she can do much better than a biker whose major skill is he can draw and paint."

"Stop selling yourself short!" she growls out.

"You been hanging around Gunner and his brothers too much, cuz," I tease. "For a second there, you sounded all growly."

"Whatever. What time are you leaving?"

"Gonna run by the shop and put a clear coat on a helmet I finished yesterday, then head on out. Gunner knows I'm coming, right?"

"Yeah, and the presidents have done whatever it is that they do so I'm supposed to let you know you can wear your colors or some shit, and your room will be ready at the clubhouse."

I smirk, even though she can't see me. I may belong to another club, but Gunner takes his position as a blood relative seriously, so by proxy, I have another club behind me. At least when I'm in town, that is.

"Then let me get off here so I can get it done and get on the road. Seems I have to figure out where I'm putting some saltwater taffy." Her squeals have me chuckling as I disconnect the call.

Most would think I was rude to do it, but Honor is well

aware of my habits by now. When I'm done talking, I hang up. Plain and simple.

"You sure you don't want one of us with you, brother?" Atlas asks as I clean up my work area.

It's one of my quirks; once I'm done with a task, everything that was used gets cleaned then stored where it belongs. I like knowing where my tools are at and since Atlas and Orion like an organized shop, it works for them as well.

"Nah, this isn't my first trip. Shouldn't have any problems whatsoever. Appreciate it, though."

"It's who we are, Glacier. Figure you should know that by now," he replies. "Come, Kobe."

I watch as his service dog follows alongside him, the two of them heading toward the office. I'm not worried about my paycheck since it's direct deposited. As I turn back to finish cleaning up, I have to shut down the thoughts wanting to intrude about how the club found me. Time enough to think about that when I'm on the open road so the wind therapy can help clear it all away once again.

Finally satisfied that everything is just where it's supposed to be, I take a few pictures of the helmet I just finished so I can show Gunner, then turn off the lights in my area. Passing the office door, I rap lightly on the jamb and call out, "See you in a week or so, brother."

"I'm sure we'll have some orders by then, Shark is taking an inventory to place an order because Roane noticed several came in to the online store."

"It keeps the gas in my girl, so I'm good with it," I reply. "Later."

After gassing up, I head inside to get Honor's saltwater taffy, a smirk on my lips. I change directions once inside, deciding to take a quick piss, then grab something to drink. Might as well take care of all the basics before I let the asphalt calm my soul.

"Don't stare, honey, it's not polite," I hear a woman say. Turning my head, I spot a little boy who reminds me of myself at that age, gawking at me.

"He's okay, ma'am," I reply, as I finish filling my drink.

"He saw you pull in on your motorcycle," she admits.

Turning, I crouch so I'm at eye level and ask, "Do you like motorcycles?"

"Oh, he doesn't talk much," she stammers, just as he opens his mouth and says, "Vroom, vroom."

His mother's gasp has me looking up at her to see tears slowly rolling down her face. "He... he's never said anything!" she whispers. "Usually just random sounds and noises, but what he just did was clear."

Standing back up and now feeling uncomfortable at the attention we're attracting, I rub my hand across the back of my neck and ask, "Does he... is he autistic by any chance?"

"How did you know?" she replies.

"Because I was slow to start talking. Maybe not as old as him, I don't really remember. I know from what my cousin has told me, they've come a long way with therapies and schooling."

"We're still searching for the right place for him. He's really smart outside of the fact he just won't talk."

"He will when he's got something important he wants to say," I tell her, ruffling the little boy's hair. I remember too late that while I'm much better about being touched, he may not be there just yet, and pull back, only to have him take hold of my hand and put it back on his head.

"I think he likes you," his mom murmurs.

"He's a cute kid. Good luck, ma'am. I have to pick a few things up then head back out."

"Safe travels, young man. And thank you for what you did today."

I shrug because I really didn't do anything special. I was just myself and it clicked with her son is all. I wave to the little boy then quickly grab several packages of peppermint as well as cinnamon saltwater taffy, pay for it all then head back to my bike. Once everything is stowed in my saddlebag, I pull my helmet on, double check that my drink is secure in its holder then turn the key, the satisfying rumble of my girl soothing a part of me that had gotten a bit unsettled inside the store.

As the miles pass away, my thoughts circle back to what life was like before the club found me.

After a few hard weeks of scrounging around, I managed to find day work, which has kept me fed and put gas in my bike, but not much else, so every night has been a struggle as I look for somewhere safe to sleep. I can't call Honor or Gunner, because my phone was stolen the first night I slept in a doorway. Thankfully, even though the asshole who stole it beat me up as well, he didn't find where I had tucked what little money I had. I'm still healing, however, and the cuts, bruises, and welts have me aching by the end of the day. All I want to do is curl up and sleep, but I need to be sure I'm safe.

A small alley ahead beckons so I carefully maneuver around the overfull dumpsters, my nose wrinkling at the stench. I'll have to ride out to the truck stop near the interstate and pay for a shower in the morning, but I had heard the men who ran the businesses didn't put up with anyone's bullshit, so I was hoping I could snag a few hours of sleep.

"I wish they had prepared us for this," I muttered as I shut my bike down then camouflaged it so it wouldn't be readily seen by anyone just passing by. "Not that I had much when I aged out, but hell, what good is it for the state to 'protect' kids by removing them from bad homes only to toss them out on the streets when they turn eighteen?"

Grabbing the tarp off the back of my bike, I pull out a bag of fast food from my saddlebag then crouch against the wall, the tarp protecting me from the elements as I quickly eat. Even though I'm in Georgia right now, the weather is bitterly cold and rainy, and I briefly wonder if maybe I should go hang out by the truck stop. If I do it just right, I can sit inside for a little while and get warmed up, then go back outside. Instead, my full belly lulls me to sleep, dreams of life I've never known teasing me.

"Fuck, brother, we can't leave him like this," a deep male voice says, dragging me from my slumber. I'm so cold and wet right now that tremors are coursing through my body. "He looks like someone beat the hell out of him."

"Trident, check him over and see if he's okay for us to take care of at the clubhouse or if we need to take him to the hospital.

Atlas, he's wearing leathers, see if you can find a bike because we'll need to take that as well."

"Don't take my bike," I stutter out, my teeth clacking together almost painfully. "It's all I got."

"Not here to hurt you, man, just want to help," another man states, crouching down on the side where my eye is so swollen, I'm unable to see him. When he realizes my dilemma, he moves slightly until I can see him. "Name's Poseidon. Our motion detectors alerted us to the fact someone was out here, but it's been glitching lately, so we didn't come right out otherwise we'd have found you sooner. You got a name?"

"Asa," I whisper, my throat raw and scratchy.

"Well, Asa, seems you need a bit of luck to go your way for a change," Poseidon says.

I snort, because the likelihood of me ever having anything besides shitty luck is slim and none at this point. I have no illusions that my quirks, as Honor calls them, push people away, but after a lifetime of being kicked around like I was trash, my ability to trust is severely limited to a select few.

"C'mon, man, you can't seriously think living on the streets is a good idea," another guy says.

I peer up at him and see he's wearing a cut like Gunner's club does; his name is Atlas, and the one who keeps checking my pulse is Trident. I don't get a bad vibe off of them, but I'm still wary as fuck right now.

"Just had a bad day is all," I finally mumble.

"One that was bad enough that your one eye is still swollen a week or so later," Trident retorts. At my shocked look, he smirks. "Too many years as a trauma nurse make me almost an expert as to how old a bruise is, Asa."

"We're wasting daylight. We've got our truck with us and can trailer your bike, but I want you out of these elements before you end up with pneumonia. You already sound like shit," Poseidon decrees.

And just like that… the Poseidon's Warriors MC saved another life.

CHAPTER FOUR

Glacier

"Do you really need to take a pic?" I ask Honor as she holds up her phone while leaning into me. "You know I hate them."

"Come on, Asa, we have to commemorate our visit," she teases. "Say 'cheese'!"

Rolling my eyes, I turn and open up my saddlebag so I can pull out the Buc-ee's bag. "Here," I say, thrusting the bag at her. It's a little fuller because she loves the stupid mascot and they had a seasonal T-shirt as well as a fuzzy throw near the register, so I grabbed those for her as well as the candy.

"Oh my God, you got me a present," she says, eagerly opening up the bag. Her squeal of excitement as me squinting as I wonder, once again, how it is that females can hit a pitch that causes ears to bleed.

"It's not a big deal, Honor," I mumble, embarrassment turning my ears red. "Just saw them as I was checking out and figured you'd like them is all."

She throws her arms around me in a bear hug, forcefully causing my breath to expel in a rush, as I wasn't expecting her actions. "You're still not getting away without us taking a picture!" she exclaims, turning around and pulling her phone out once again as she leans into my side.

The first one, I flip off the camera, a scowl on my face, which has her elbowing me in the gut. "Ouch, stop it, brat!"

"Then quit fucking around," she sasses. "Now, smile, Asa."

This time, I smirk which makes her sigh in defeat. "Fine. Someday, when I'm showing my kids pics of us, they're going to ask what's wrong with your face."

"Why would they do that?" I ask.

"Because in every picture I have of us as adults, you're either scowling, glowering, snarling, or flipping off the camera!" she retorts, her hand on her hip as she glares at me.

I can't help it, I burst out laughing while pulling her in again. "Take another one, Honor, I promise I won't fuck this one up."

She quickly takes several pictures before stepping back and looking at them. "Much, much better. How can I get her interested in you if you look like a serial killer wannabe?" she mutters to herself.

"What the hell?"

"Um, nothing. Now, where are we going to eat? I know my brother plans to hog some of your time, but I get you until later, right? Can we go shopping?"

"Whatever will fit in the saddlebags, Honor," I warn. "Remember what happened the last time."

"Oh yeah," she replies, giggling. "Gunner wasn't happy that he had to send a prospect to pick up all the stuff I wanted. Maybe we should just get something to eat, and I'll wait for Delaney to get back into town to fulfill my retail therapy needs."

"Sounds like a plan. You choose where we're going."

"Really like the helmet, Glacier," Gunner says as we walk back into the clubhouse after our ride.

"I like it as well," I reply, following him over to the bar where he calls for a prospect to bring us a few beers.

"Y'all selling them or is it just something you're doing for your club?" he questions.

"We sell 'em now, Gun," I say after taking a long pull from my drink.

"Gonna take this to the brothers, see if they want to get some," he replies, smirking at me. "Keeping you busy means you can't get into trouble."

"When have I ever gotten into trouble?" I retort.

He shrugs, sucking down the rest of his beer. "It could happen. So, what did my sister want to do?"

"She *wanted* me to take her shopping, but I wasn't driving a cage and reminded her of what happened the last time I took her. So instead, we went to dinner. She seems to like her job, doesn't she?" I ask.

Part of me wishes her roommate had been here this time; I really want to meet this woman whose pictures have captivated me. I push away thoughts of the bitch who destroyed me in high school. I'm still not ready to commit my life to anyone, much less a woman, but maybe, just maybe, with what she does for a living, she'd be okay with someone like me.

One can always hope, right?

CHAPTER FIVE

Glacier

Stretching to get the kinks out of my back, I hear my phone chime, then notice everyone grabbing their phones from their pockets. Having finally found my niche with the club, which is at the auto shop where I handle the detailed paint jobs, I idly wonder if we have a new order or something.

I grab my phone and see one word in all caps from Poseidon, our club president.

Church.

I shut down the compressor I use for the airbrush and toss my gloves on the workbench before pulling off the coveralls that protect my clothes from the paints. I had already taken the helmet off; it has a built-in respirator so I'm not constantly breathing in fumes. Once I'm sure my work area is good to go, I head out to my bike then crank her up, grinning at the way she sounds. With a nod at Atlas, who will lock up the shop before he follows us, I head toward our clubhouse, which is a little way out of town, relishing the salty smell in the air as the wind comes in along the coast.

Best thing Poseidon ever did was move us further down the coast of Georgia as far as I'm concerned. I didn't have any real say-so then as I was just a prospect, but for me, putting more distance from my past helped settle something deep inside.

"So, Gunner from the DRMC reached out after seeing Glacier's helmet. He and his club placed an order. They'd like you to deliver them, Brother," Poseidon states, looking at me.

"Not a problem, Pres," I reply. "Haven't seen them in a few months, guess it's time again before Honor starts blowing up my phone."

I grin because she's like a rabid dog with a bone sometimes, always wanting me to 'zip up and see her'. Sadly, I've been so busy that it's been longer than I like, but this will be the perfect opportunity.

"Honor? Who's that?" Trident asks, smirking at me.

"Gunner's sister, which makes her my cousin as well," I retort.

"Fuck, I was hoping it was a woman you've kept hidden from us," Trident murmurs.

After the shit I went through my junior year in high school? Yeah, no. Never falling for a woman again. Besides, none of them would ever want a freak like me.

Except you've become obsessed with meeting Delaney, my brain whispers.

"I hear you're coming to visit! It's been forever, Asa," Honor squeals through the phone. "I can't wait to *finally* introduce you to my roommate, Delaney."

Pulling the phone away from my ear because I'm pretty sure she just ruptured my eardrum with her screaming, I roll my eyes even though she can't see me. I know she's trying to fix me up with this Delaney chick, but I no longer do commitments or relationships. Nope. Junior year and Bethany Jayne Northrup cured me of wanting forever with anyone. When my thoughts try to remind me of how often I stare at Delaney's picture, I quickly shut that shit down. I know I'd *like* to have what so many of my brothers have found, but that doesn't mean she'd want to get involved with the likes of me; a biker with a shitty past. Still, to appease my cousin, I'll meet her roommate.

There's always hope, my inner self whispers. *Don't throw away the possibility of a happily ever after.*

"Be glad to meet her, squirt," I tease. "Need to make sure your brother isn't losing his touch about allowing undesirables into your life."

"Don't call me squirt!" she retorts. "That's almost as bad as when you call me brat! Besides, Delaney's a good one, Asa, she really is. She grew up like us, and is now a special education teacher at our elementary school."

"They didn't have those when we were coming up, did they?" I muse. "Not really, I mean, I know they had a classroom where kids who were disabled were at, but no clue what they were actually taught."

"Sure would have helped," she agrees. "Between my ADHD and your autism, we needed someone who would have our backs."

"Instead, we spent a lot of time in ISS," I say. "At least we got our homework wrapped up, right?"

"True, but we managed to figure out how to make things work, didn't we, Asa?"

"Yeah, Honor, we did."

"So, when will you be here?" she asks, excitement returning to her tone.

"As soon as all the helmets are finished," I promise. "I'll take you and your roommate out to dinner, okay, squirt?"

"I can't wait!" she enthuses, nearly shattering my eardrum. Again.

"Same here."

Chapter Six

Nearly One Month Later

Glacier

"H'lo?" My voice is raspy since the ringing phone pulled me from a sound sleep.

"A-a-asa?" The stuttering, tear-filled voice has me immediately alert and I sit up in bed, before switching my phone to speaker so I can get dressed.

"Honor? What's the matter, honey?" I ask after seeing who's calling on the caller ID, all while grabbing my jeans from the end of the bed and slipping them on. "Talk to me," I demand when all she does is cry.

She's been my closest friend since we were in the system together, not realizing when we first met that we were cousins. Two outcasts who quickly learned who they could and couldn't rely on. After I got her to Gunner and started trying to make my own way in life, we didn't see or talk to each other all that often, but that's changed. It's been almost two months since I've last seen her because of work obligations, but once the helmets are finished drying then packed up and put in the truck, I'll be heading up to the clubhouse and will be taking her and her roommate out to dinner. Although I haven't yet met Delaney in person, I've heard so much about her that I feel as though I already know her.

"She... she's gone. They took her."

"Who's gone?" I growl out, now grabbing clothes and throwing them into my duffel bag. I'm already scheduled to make a run up to the DRMC with the load of custom helmets later this week since they're finally all finished, but if someone Honor cares about is missing, I'll hit the road a little sooner than I planned. Poseidon is just gonna have to understand.

"Honor is, this is Delaney," the female finally replies. It's then that I'm awake enough to realize I'm talking to Honor's roommate, not Honor herself.

"Shit, fuck, dammit," I growl out, pissed at myself for mistaking the two womens' voices. "I just talked to her yesterday since I'm finally headed in that direction this week with shit for the club. How do you know she's missing?" I ask.

I hear her sigh before she admits, "Honor has Type 1 diabetes but didn't want her brother to know. She and I have a system where she checks in with me so when she didn't call or text me, I drove up to her job and found her car right where she always parks. Asa, her kit's still in it, along with her cellphone. The app I have to help track things with regard to her sugar shows it's steadily rising, which isn't good."

"Why not? I don't understand what you mean," I rumble, grabbing my bag and heading out of my suite of rooms.

"Okay, so her goal is to keep her sugar levels somewhat consistent. She has an insulin pump which automatically injects her with insulin to keep them that way, but if she's stressed or hurt, her fight or flight instinct kicks in and it causes havoc. If they're too high for too long, it can cause her to go into a diabetic coma. She can *die*, Asa," Delaney cries out, now sobbing again.

"Get to the Devil's Riot MC clubhouse, I'm on my way and will call Gunner to apprise him of the situation," I order, practically running to where the truck I was taking is sitting, my bike already loaded in the back, along with the helmets. Well, I hope the fucking helmets are all in there; if not, one of the guys can bring them up. Right now, it's not my fucking priority; Honor is.

The original plan was that I'd leave later this week since I had a few things to wrap up at the shop, but this changes everything and while I'm sure he'll be pissed, Poseidon will understand. I just hope Atlas will, although he's mellowed out a lot since his daughter was born.

"I couldn't get Gunner, he didn't answer the phone when I called," Delaney advises.

"He'll talk to me," I retort, tossing my bag into the back seat of the truck before carefully laying my cut on the passenger seat. "Just head there, Delaney. I'll be there as soon as I can get there, and we'll find her."

The last thing I hear before she hangs up is a whispered, "I hope so."

"Poseidon, I've left for South Carolina," I say once he answers the phone.

"Brother, it's like four in the fucking morning," he growls out, his voice raspy with sleep. "Besides, you were leaving in a few days, not today. What changed?"

"My cousin's missing."

After all this time, he's used to my abruptness. I say what I have to say and not much more. It's easier than explaining my quirkiness to other people and with what I learned years ago, it's just better. My brothers are all fucked up in their own ways, so they take my personality in stride. Outsiders aren't as understanding, which is why I'm grateful as hell I found the club. Well, more like, I'm grateful they found *me*.

"Need me to call Gunner and let him know you're on your way?" he asks, sounding more alert now.

"No, this call needs to come from me. Will you let Atlas know I was nearly done with the Benson project? Actually, the artwork is all done, it only needs the clear coat applied. Was going to wrap that up before I left, but I want to be up there to help find her."

"Gotcha. You be sure to let Gunner know I can send more brothers up to help have y'all's backs."

I snicker at his words which has him barking out, "What? Why does that make you laugh?"

"Brother, I suspect some of his club thinks we're nothing but a bunch of pussies," I admit.

"Why the fuck would they think something like that?"

"Because we're legit," I reply, as if it should make sense.

"Jesus Fucking Christ, you're kidding me, right?" he retorts.

"Nope. Overheard one of them saying it when I called back to confirm the details of the helmets."

"They know our background?" Poseidon questions.

"Y'mean how most of y'all are former Navy SEALS? Highly decorated? Hold records?" I ask. "It's never come up in conversation, so I've never mentioned it."

"I see. I'll get Trident, Brooks, and Atlas headed in that direction with me," he advises before hanging up.

Fuck. The best hope I have is that Gunner will appreciate the extra hands looking for Honor. Otherwise, my family connection may get severed if my president orders no further contact.

"Dammit, Gunner, answer the motherfucking phone," I growl out, hanging up once again when it rolls to voicemail.

I realize it's not even six in the morning now, and he's a biker to boot, but I know if I woke up to ten missed calls from the same person, I'd fucking call them back. The light indicating the truck needs gas illuminates so I start looking for an exit where I can kill multiple birds with one stone.

Gas, piss, coffee, and maybe a gas station breakfast sandwich.

When I spot the road sign indicating there's a Love's station two miles ahead, I grin. Out of all the stations in our neck of the woods, they're my personal favorite. They usually have either a Hardee's or a Carl's Jr. inside for food, but barring that, they have a wide selection of snack-type foods I can grab as well. Fuck it, might as well fill up my insulated bag with ice, drinks, and snacks, because I've still got about seven or so hours left on this drive, and I don't want to stop unless absolutely necessary.

After making sure the truck is locked, I start pumping gas, then head inside to take care of the rest of my list. It's one of my quirks; I will focus on something until it's completed. Most of my mental lists are short; some are much longer, and are repeated frequently depending on the task I need to accomplish.

Honor and I found this helped keep me on track with school, as well as life. Before that, I would spiral, get angry and lash out, or throw tantrums that would rival a two-year-old's.

DARLENE TALLMAN

Thankfully, the store isn't all that busy and I'm able to grab everything I want for my insulated cooler, along with a freshly made breakfast biscuit. Just hope like hell I can get Gunner soon. Every minute counts as far as I'm concerned, especially now knowing Honor's secret.

Yeah, I'm reaming her out for that one too, as soon as she's safe, that is. All of us, *especially* her brother, should've known about her condition. What if she had had a problem one day when she was around the club? None of them would've known what the hell to do for her.

As I make my way back to my truck, I mutter, "You're so in trouble, squirt. Gonna beat your ass if your brother doesn't beat me to it."

With my stuff now stowed in my cooler, I put the gas nozzle up, grab my receipt so I can be reimbursed once I get home, then get back on the road, praying like hell that Gunner answers the fucking phone.

Two hours and nearly one hundred or so miles later, I *finally* get an answer.

"I'm in Church, motherfucker. What the fuck are you doing blowing up my phone?" Gunner snarls.

"Honor's missing."

Dead silence. As in, the background noise I was hearing suddenly dissipates.

"Say that again? You're now on speaker," he advises, his voice now sounding deadly.

I shiver at his tone, but feel the same way because whoever took her has bought themselves an unmarked grave preceded by a shit ton of torture. "Honor's missing, man. Her roommate called me a few hours ago and I hit the road. Been trying to get you for a bit, didn't you see the missed calls?"

"No, I didn't see you called. It was in the room charging. Zinnia just burst into Church and told me you were callin'," he says. "What, exactly, did Delaney tell you?"

Sighing deeply because I know I'm about to blow his mind, I reply, "Apparently, Honor's been keeping a secret from all of us except for Delaney. She's got Type 1 diabetes, Gunner, and the two of them have a system to make sure it stays on track."

Voices immediately start talking over one another before I can finish what I'm saying. "Shut the fuck up, and let him talk!" Gunner bellows.

"Delaney explained that she has some app on her phone that will indicate when there's a problem with Honor's sugar levels. It did and she drove to the hospital and found her car unlocked. The only thing is, Honor never made it inside for her shift, and her cellphone as well as her testing kit were still in the passenger seat."

"How did Delaney know to call *you*?" he questions.

"Apparently, when you didn't answer her calls, she went to the last person Honor talked to, which was me," I retort. "I'm also listed as one of her ICE contacts still, even though I'm not exactly right next door."

"Son of a bitch, she tried calling me five times and you called twenty?" he yells. "What shift is she on right now? When did you get your call?"

"She was working from seven at night until seven in the morning," I reply. "Delaney called me between two and three, not one hundred percent sure, just know I threw clothes in my bag and hit the road close to four. Wait, I told her to head to the clubhouse since I knew it'd take me roughly eight hours or so to get there. Are you saying she's not there?" I question, worry for her now added to my concern for my cousin.

"No, she's not and it's not like she's never been here before. She was here the other day for Delilah's birthday party with Honor. Hammer?" Gunner asks, referring to his president to presumably have some guys go look for Delaney.

I hear another voice command, "Dagger, Glock, Ruger, I want you to head out and look for Delaney."

"What's she drive?" a voice asks.

"Gunner, you know?" Hammer replies.

"A blue Volkswagen Bug," Gunner states. "And before anyone gets any stupid fucking ideas, I know because she's my damn sister's roommate and I try to keep an eye on them. Little good that did me. Didn't even know my damn sister was a diabetic."

"Got it, Gun," the unknown male responds. "We'll let you know what we find."

A bunch of noise comes across the line, irritating my pounding head, but I wait for Gunner or even Hammer to speak.

"How much longer before you get here?" Gunner asks.

"Maybe about five hours, give or take. Just gassed up so it's unlikely I'll have to again. Oh, and be prepared, Poseidon is sending up Trident, Atlas, and Brooks to assist in the search."

"We don't need those pussies, we can find Honor ourselves," a new voice loudly retorts.

I debate whether or not to say anything, then decide to forge ahead. "You know they're former SEALS, right?"

"Fuuuuuck," Gunner quietly says. "You mean to tell me a bunch of motherfucking badasses are legit? They could've done anything, and no one would've fucked with them!"

"They went legit because Poseidon wanted to honor his grandfather, but make no mistakes, they're not men to fuck with," I advise, barely holding back my chuckle.

"Then we'll gladly take their help," Hammer asserts.

"Good, because Brooks actually handles our skip traces and shit now."

"Well, get here, Glacier," Gunner demands.

"Be there as soon as I can," I promise before hanging up.

CHAPTER SEVEN

Delaney

"Stupid deer family," I cry out while smacking my steering wheel.

After hanging up with Asa, I made sure I had Honor's things and locked up her car, then started driving to the clubhouse. Unfortunately for me, I didn't see the three deer crossing the road until I was hit by two of them and then struck the last one, which caused me to run off the road into a tree. I'm pretty sure I blacked out when my airbags deployed all around me, if the missing time is any indication.

I'd try to call Gunner again, but he hasn't answered any of my other calls, so I decide not to bother. Instead, I open up my roadside assistance app and prepare to call for help from them.

When I catch a glimpse of myself in the rearview mirror, I can't help the moan that passes my lips. The left side of my face is bruised, and my nose has dried blood underneath it that is covering my shirt as well. My head is pounding, and my vision is double right now as well. Fuck my life!

"You look like the walking dead," I mutter to myself. "Well, no help for it. Get your ass out of the car and start walking. Honor needs you, bitch! You can always try calling Gunner again and maybe this time, he'll answer the damn phone."

After locking up my car, I start walking, only to realize my shirt's covered in blood. While I don't want to waste time, I also don't want to scare anyone, so I head to the trunk where I keep my gym bag and am digging around inside to see what I can change into when I hear the unmistakable sound of several motorcycles getting close to where I'm parked.

"You're making such a fashion statement, girlie," I tell myself after I catch a glimpse in the side mirror. Because I expected to find Honor at the hospital working away, I wore my old, almost threadbare sweatpants, a pair of flip-flops, and a t-shirt, with my hair piled up on the top of my head. Hell, I'm still wearing the readers I had on because I was in the middle of grading papers! I fell asleep around midnight and when my phone alerted me to a problem, I headed to the hospital to see if I could figure out what was going on. Normally, she texts or calls me when she gets there, which she didn't do, but sometimes, an emergency comes in and she's not able to, so I didn't worry too much.

Until the app went off. I know she never arrived for her shift, which I don't remember whether or not I told Asa, because I went inside with the excuse she had forgotten her lunch only to be told she wasn't there. That's when I went to her car and found her cellphone and started trying to call her brother. Thank God Asa answered his phone because I'm unsure how to go about finding her at this point.

Asa must've gotten in touch with Gunner and since I'm not where he told me to be, I suspect Gunner sent some of the other men to come find me.

Three bikes pull up around my car and one of the guys gets off while the other two sit there staring at me. All three are intimidating as hell, but I remind myself that in a way, they're Honor's family since Gunner's a part of their club.

I turn and stare back, not giving that first fuck that I'm a hot mess. "Jesus Christ," one of them says, his tone harsh. "What the fuck happened to you?"

"If you think I look bad, you should see the other guy," I reply.

"You Delaney?" the biker who's now approaching me asks. At my nod, he replies, "Name's Ruger. Looks like you had a bit of fun this morning."

I can't help it, my sass shows up as I retort, "If that's what you want to call it. I call it stupid nature. I saw them, even slowed down and missed the first two but that last one decided to hit me anyhow. How can I possibly let my kids see me looking like this?"

"You got kids?" the guy on the left questions. "Damn shame."

"I'm a teacher," I say. "I don't have any kids of my own."

Yet.

I leave that part unsaid. I'd love to find a man who would accept me warts and all as my granny used to say but sadly, they're few and far between. I'm barely over five feet tall, with blonde hair that tends to curl despite my best efforts. Oh, and let's not forget that even though I work out religiously, my love for chocolate ripple ice cream with sprinkles means my abs will always be encased in a layer of pudge. Most of the men I've dated end up breaking up with me because I'm nowhere near a size two and have zero plans to get there. Plus, I tend to speak my mind and am what one of my former boyfriends called 'free spirited and sassy'. Whatever.

Life is meant to be lived and enjoyed. Chaining myself to a miserable existence eating baked chicken and broccoli all the time is never going to be in my wheelhouse. And if a man can't grasp that fact, he can just jump off a pier as far as I'm concerned.

"Gunner wants you at the clubhouse. Are you hurt beyond what I can see?" Ruger asks, breaking into my reverie.

"I'm sure I'll be a little sore in the next few days, but other than that, I'm good."

"Get on my bike," he demands. "You can clean up there if you want. Seems we need to get all the information possible so we can find Honor."

CHAPTER EIGHT

Glacier

After what seems like forever, I pull into the parking lot of the DRMC's clubhouse. I'm barely out of the truck when I see Gunner stalking toward me. "Get inside, we've got a plan of action," he demands.

I nod and fall into step with him as he turns and heads to the door which is being held open by someone I presume is a prospect. As we breach the doorway, I spy a woman in a tank top and sweatpants sitting off to the side, a glass of something between her hands.

A man sitting at the head of the table approaches me and holds out his hand. "Name's Hammer, President of the Devil's Riot MC, Southeast Charter."

"Glacier here, glad to meet you but hate the circumstances," I reply, shaking his hand.

Hammer motions for everyone, including me and the woman sitting near the bar, to gather around the tables that appear to have been pushed together. I suspect if this discussion didn't include me and the girl, they'd likely be talking about it in Church, like we would at home. Glancing around, I don't see anyone milling about, like ol' ladies or club girls, so I make a note to ask Gunner later if it crosses my mind.

"Have a seat. My guys found Delaney not far from here. Seems she and a few deer had a battle of sorts and she lost," Hammer says.

I glance over at the woman to see a blush covering her bruised face. "You okay?" I quietly ask, something drawing me to her.

Years have passed since a woman has captivated me; that's not to say I haven't enjoyed my fair share, but I don't do relationships, so it's usually a one-off kind of thing whenever my hand stops doing the job.

"I will be as soon as we find Honor," she says, worrying her bottom lip.

Once everyone has been introduced and we're seated around the tables, Hammer puts his fingers between his lips and shrilly whistles, causing the small murmured conversations to cease. "Honor, Gunner's sister, is missing and we're gonna presume one of our enemies has taken her. The bigger issue is apparently, for those who didn't know, she's a diabetic and her levels are going up or some shit."

I watch Gunner's face and know he's equal parts livid and scared for his sister. Leaning toward him, I whisper, "She shoulda told you."

Hell, I'm surprised she never told me seeing as we talk about virtually everything. Thanks to my beloved cousin, I know more about a woman's time of the month than I ever wanted to, although a smirk plays across my lips when I remember her telling me that I'd make someone very happy someday. Something about knowing when to pull out the heating pad and buy chocolate or some shit.

"Yeah, she should have but I suspect she figured I would take some of her independence away if I knew," he grumbles. I know I'd feel the same way, so maybe that's why she kept quiet with me as well.

"Those of you who are members, we know we're at a standstill with the De La Rosa Cartel and as for Avery's siblings, those fuckwads are a pain in the ass. This being said, although one is more of a nuisance while the other is an all-out war, we've got to figure out if either of them have anything to do with this shit. We've already ruled out the Senator's son," Hammer remarks, looking around the table. "If I had to take a wild guess though, between the two, this shit stinks more of those bastards that share blood with my woman. The De La Rosas, although they'd go after a woman, they'd want us to know it was them," Hammer growls out.

"They don't always, Prez," Ruger replies. "Could be either one of them."

"We need to get out there and check out their last known whereabouts," Glock calls out.

I nod in agreement even though I am completely ignorant of both situations they're talking about, because time is of the essence. My gut tightens when I see Delaney's face blanche after she glances at her phone. Somehow, without her saying a word, I instinctively know that something's going on with Honor's diabetes.

———⋹———

We've been going back and forth for about thirty minutes when suddenly, Delaney raises her hand, which has me biting my cheek to keep from grinning. At Hammer's grunt in her direction, she shrilly says, "Something has to get done soon. Her pump is dying."

"What the fuck does that mean?" Gunner asks, his body tensing even more than it already was. I may not always pick up on social cues and shit, but he's coiled so tightly right now, I almost expect his head to explode.

"It means that soon, it won't be working so her body won't be getting the insulin it needs. If she's not found in the next few hours, she could wind up in a diabetic coma and possibly die," Delaney retorts.

I'm impressed that despite being surrounded by men who are large, muscled, and tattooed, she's not acting all that intimidated. It's possible, of course, that she's too afraid for my cousin to worry about it, but most women wouldn't have the guts to say what she just did in the tone she used. Especially not with this crew. While at the end of the day they're a brotherhood, there's no mistaking the fact that they're worlds apart from the club I call home. They're harder, more intimidating, and give off a 'don't fuck with me vibe' that my brothers typically only pull out when the situation warrants it. I suspect the DRMC wears it all the time, just like they wear their cuts.

Surprisingly, no one blows up at her. Instead, Hammer gives Gunner a look that I interpret to mean he needs to calm his shit while nodding to Delaney.

"Cy, get some drones up and going to check out Avery's siblings' hideouts," Hammer orders.

"On it, Prez," Cy replies, fingers flying across the keyboard. Having watched Specks do this at home, I'm impressed when he looks at Hammer and says, "Done."

"What about the cartel?" Glock questions. "We really can't discount them."

"We'll look into them, but let's rule out the siblings first," Hammer replies. "I can feel it in my gut they're behind this shit."

"Don't they have that shack not too far from here?" Axe asks. "I mean, it's not like they're that intelligent, so if it *is* them, they wouldn't think to run far away from us."

"They're not that intelligent and they'll do whatever they can to get back at Avery and the club. It would be just like them to have her right under our noses," Hammer says, nodding.

"I'm going to check it out," Gunner emphatically advises.

Hammer looks around the table and says, "Savage, Dagger, Axe, y'all three come with us. Dagger, make sure you've got your bag."

"Take her kit with you," Delaney states, thrusting it in Gunner's direction. "There's a bottle of insulin and some syringes, along with her testing kit, so you can give her some. She's gonna need it."

Gunner looks green at the thought of giving his sister a shot and immediately hands it over to Dagger, who smirks. "I'll handle it, Brother," he says, looking inside the kit to see what all is inside.

"Now that that's settled, let's head out," Hammer decrees, slamming the gavel. "The rest of you wait here because I'm sure we'll have something to take care of if she's there."

While part of me wishes I was helping with my cousin's rescue, I suspect the woman currently leaning against me, needs help as well.

And maybe I'm just the man to provide it.

Because Honor was right; I *do* like her roommate. At least what I've seen so far.

CHAPTER NINE

Delaney

I'm kind of glad most of the men have left, because I'm not gonna lie, they all scare the everloving hell out of me. I might have acted like I wasn't scared, but years of dealing with over-the-top parents has given me the ability to hide my feelings. At least until I'm by myself, that is; then I typically fall apart and either rant and rave or cry.

Except the man they've been calling Glacier, who is Honor's cousin. He's not as tall or as muscular as the other men, although he's still intimidating in his own right. He doesn't talk much either, which I notice rather quickly as we sit around a table closer to the bar. The silence doesn't bother me; I'd prefer not to fill the air with meaningless chatter, especially when I'm beyond worried about my best friend right now. Even my own aches and pains are taking a backseat, at least until she's found.

I sip on a soda while he peels the label off the beer he got from a woman working behind the bar. I'm not all that familiar with motorcycle clubs, but from her attire, I presume she's what they would refer to as a club whore. Not that I'd ever judge another person's choices, because I sure as heck won't, but I know for myself I could never live that kind of life. I want one man, preferably for the rest of my days, as many kids as he'll give me, and maybe a few pets.

"How's it looking now?" Glacier suddenly asks, drawing my attention away from my thoughts and to him.

I look at my phone and groan. "They've gone up again," I quietly state. "I really hope they find her soon."

Before he can answer, the door opens, and four men walk in who draw the attention of the rest of the club members who are hanging around like Hammer instructed.

"Glacier, you haven't unloaded those helmets yet?" one of the men questions, his focus on the biker sitting close to me.

"Fuck off, Atlas," Glacier grumbles. "Got bigger issues right now."

"Yeah, we heard. Any news yet?" the man he called Atlas asks.

"They've got a search party out now," Glacier replies. "I guess we could unload the stuff while we wait for them to get back."

"Naw, we'll have a prospect do it," Glock retorts. "That's what they're here for, to do the shit stuff."

"Let me get my bike off," Glacier says, "then they can have at it."

I watch as he heads toward the men, they do that weird man-hug shit, then they walk out the door, several other guys following closely behind. I want to fan my face because despite the seriousness of the situation, Glacier is making me feel things I've never had happen to me before.

Regardless of the fact we've barely spoken, I can see a future with him, which is absolutely absurd to me. Granted, Honor has extolled his virtues to me for years, but until today, we've always missed out on meeting each other when he makes a trip up to see her. Hell, he lives in a completely different state, while I'm settled here with a job, an apartment, and a relatively good life. Of course, the day I finally *do* meet him, I'm bruised up from my run-in with the deer and dressed like a vagrant. Sigh. Such is my damn luck.

Okay, so the local dating pool sucks. Most of the men I've been out with are just looking to get into my panties, something I'm unwilling to do. It's one of the things Honor and I initially had in common when we first met; we were both virgins. She, of course, has eliminated her V-card after a night with Savage, the man she wants with everything in her. He's being a douche, though, and won't fight for what's right in front of him. Maybe all of that will change once they find and rescue her. Providing her health crisis doesn't kill her, that is. Shaking my head at my macabre thoughts, I wait for the men to return, worry for my best friend keeping me from focusing on any one thing.

Once again, I'm surrounded by bikers, but this time, they're from Glacier's club, Poseidon's Warriors MC. Glacier's now wearing his cut, which he must've put on when he got his bike off the truck. They seem like nice enough guys, and I've ooo'd and ahh'd over pictures of some of the cutest kids I've ever seen. Still, I'm a bit cautious simply because in my mind, there's no way someone like me would fit into their world. Just from what they've shared, their women are forces to be reckoned with, while I'm just me. A nerdy homebody who derives enjoyment from the simpler things in life.

Which is a crying shame because the more I'm around Glacier, the more I like him. He's quiet but watchful, and that's something I find myself enjoying. He's not constantly trying to fill in the silence with small talk, unlike most of the men I've dated in the past. I don't need a man who's the life of the party if I'm truly honest. I need one who is committed to me as well as our relationship.

"So, what do you do for a living?" Poseidon asks during a lull in the conversation.

"I'm a special education teacher," I reply, nervously twisting my hands in my lap.

"You help kids who struggle in school or something?" Atlas questions.

"In a nutshell, that's a good way to put it. I specialize in teaching children with physical, mental, emotional, or learning disabilities. My team and I develop teaching plans specific to each child's individual needs, working with their parents and other staff, so that the student is able to achieve important learning milestones," I reply. Then, because I'm nervous, I giggle a bit before continuing. "I mean, that kind of sounds like a rote response, but it's actually not. My current student load is only five children, but each kid has a different teaching plan based on their challenges, so even though the average classroom has between twenty and thirty kids, my five keep me on my toes just as well as a 'full' class would."

"That would've been great to have when I was a kid," Glacier quietly remarks.

"What do you mean?" I ask him. His face turns ruddy, and I realize I've embarrassed him. Reaching over, I lightly touch his arm and quietly say, "It's okay, you don't have to tell me if you don't want to."

He looks to his club brothers before nodding slightly. "No, it's okay. I've never gotten the actual testing, but I'm on the spectrum, but until one of my foster parents followed up with something I was told as a kid and mentioned it to the school, then one of my teachers figured it out in seventh or eighth grade, school was hell for me. Not because I couldn't learn, it's just that if it didn't interest me, I didn't care. Drove my teachers absolutely nuts. Art, math, science, they all came easy as hell to me. English, social sciences? Not so much."

"I get it. Kids on the spectrum, depending on where they fall, have varying challenges. Most who have a milder form, which it sounds like you've got, are highly intelligent, but tend to get hyper focused on things that intrigue or interest them. They also can have sensory issues, tend to miss social cues so are often bullied for being 'awkward' or 'weird'," I tell the group, who are avidly listening to me right now. I'm not one for being in the spotlight, so I can feel my face flushing at the attention they're all paying me. Well, except for Glacier, who hasn't raised his head since Poseidon asked what I did for a living.

"Yeah, sounds about right," he mutters, looking at his hands.

My heart goes out to him, wishing I could take the pain I can tell he's feeling away. Before I can say anything else, the door bursts open and most of the men who left to search for Honor come storming inside.

"We found her, she's on the way to the hospital with Gunner and Savage," Hammer states once he's closer.

"I want to see her," I demand, standing to my full height.

Inside, I cringe when I realize I'm well over a foot shorter than any of the men currently standing around, looking as though they want to rip someone's head off. However, in the scheme of things, it's irrelevant how tall or short I am; my girl needs me and I'm gonna be there for her, plain and simple.

Hammer moves closer to me, eliciting a grumble from Glacier, who gets so close to me, I can feel his body heat radiating from him. He glances at Glacier, his brow raised and a smirk on his lips before looking at me and saying, "It's bad, sweetheart. You may wanna wait until they call us."

I'm already shaking my head. "Wrong answer. I'm going whether or not I have to walk up there. She's my best friend, I need to be there." Seeing he's about to refuse, I add, "Please? Regardless of what happened to her, it doesn't matter to me at all. But she's bound to be scared when she wakes up and I want to be there for her. She'd do it for me, Hammer." Turning, I look at Glacier and can see the rage pouring off him. "Hammer? *Please?*" I plead, looking back at him as Glacier's hand tightens on my arm. I'll probably have bruises but right now, I know he's trying to keep from losing his shit, so it's a small price to pay.

Glacier's hand on my arm has me turning to him. "How about this, I'll take you up there so you can see her and ease your mind," he says, peering down at me.

"Okay. Um, can you take me by our apartment first? I need to change, and I'd like to get some of her things she's going to need."

He nods and I let out the breath I was holding before tuning in to what Hammer is now saying.

"I know you guys don't know the area all that well, but would appreciate it if the three of you rode with my guys so we can track those fuckers down," he growls out. At their looks, he continues. "It was bad. Worse than I imagined. Not sure how she's going to come back from what they've done to her."

Fuck. Knowing Honor the way that I do, I suspect this will devastate her. She won't want everyone knowing what happened, and since the people who snatched her appear to have a particular reputation, each of these men she calls family is going to know what was done to her, including Savage. My heart sinks, but I mentally shake off my doom and gloom thoughts. Whatever she needs me to do so she comes back to herself, I'll be there for her.

Every step of the way.

"You ready?" Glacier asks, lightly touching my arm again.

"Yes."

CHAPTER TEN

Glacier

Since I had the box truck and my bike, which isn't set up for a passenger, Hammer handed me a set of keys to his truck, while my brothers followed him and his brothers out to find the motherfuckers who hurt my cousin. I don't have any illusions that we'll be able to 'help' them take care of business, so I need to let Gunner know to take a few shots on my behalf in case they choose to handle it 'in house' without us in attendance. I just hope like hell when they catch up to them, they make it hurt ten times worse than whatever Honor endured.

After Delaney gave me their address, she started looking out the window, leaving me to my own tortuous thoughts, which immediately go back to my junior year in high school and Bethany Jayne Northrup.

"Oh, Asa, you look so handsome today," she purred, walking up to where I was standing at my locker to grab my book for English. Glancing down at myself, I smirk. Since when are jeans, cowboy boots, and a flannel shirt the height of fashion? Honor passes by me and raises her brow, causing me to shrug. I don't know what game Bethany is playing, but she's good at them and I refuse to get caught in her snare.

"Just my normal clothes," I replied, slamming my locker closed. "Whatcha need, Bethany? Won't Derek get mad at you for talking to another guy?"

Her boyfriend, Derek Appleby, has been one of my worst tormentors for years, so if he were to find us talking, even innocently, I'm concerned I'll earn another suspension for fighting.

"We broke up last week, Asa. Figured you would have heard," she replied, smiling at me while placing her hand on my arm and lightly squeezing.

"Nope, been busy," I retorted.

"Are you going to the dance next month?" she asked, batting her false eyelashes at me.

"Hadn't really decided," I said. If I did go, it would be with Honor since she was my best friend. I didn't really date

because I was awkward as hell around other people, especially girls.

"I'd uh... I'd love it if you'd take me," she stated, biting her pouty lip.

Bethany was a beautiful girl, but she knew it. Long blonde hair, banging hot body with perky tits, tanned skin, and legs that I had fantasized about being wrapped around my waist as I fucked her hard. She was also way out of my league because no one wanted to be seen with 'the freak' as I was called.

Couldn't blame them; I got tongue-tied when I was nervous, hadn't quite filled into my size fourteen shoe so I was gawky as hell, and since I didn't play sports, I wasn't stacked with muscles.

"You would?" I questioned, shocked.

"Yes, I've always had a secret crush on you," she replied, smiling up at me.

My heart started beating fast and I could feel a bead of sweat roll down my back as I thought about what this could mean for me.

No more being ostracized.

No more being bullied.

Instead, I'd be the envy of every guy in the school if she were on my arm.

"Then I'll take you," I advised.

For the next three weeks, I was in seventh heaven. Bethany hung on me when we walked around school, and was generous with her kisses and touches, although she only let me go so far. However, her promise of a 'night I'd never forget' every time we discussed the dance had me positive that I'd be sliding into that hot, tight body.

Whenever I wasn't with her, I was doing odd jobs in order to buy her corsage and rent myself a tux complete with a vest that matched the color of her dress. Long hours were spent in my bed, my cock in hand as I thought of all the ways I'd fuck her that night. I had already reserved a hotel room for that night, and while Honor was positive there was something nefarious going on, she agreed to cover for the fact I was going to be gone from our foster home all night long.

After getting copies of the room key early, I handed one off to Bethany because she said she had to run by her house to get a few things. She asked that I get a bottle of champagne so we could celebrate properly, then told me she'd meet me there.

Anxious because it had taken me longer to obtain the alcohol than I thought it would, I flashed my key card against the door and stepped inside.

Only to be met with Bethany and Derek, naked in the room I rented, fucking. When she spotted me, she started laughing, the sound sending shockwaves through my system.

"Did you really think I would fuck you?" she sneered. "You're nothing but a freak, Asa, and everyone knows it. But we needed a room for the night, and you fell right into our plans."

"But... but... you kissed me!" I exclaimed.

"Kisses mean nothing," she retorted.

"Now scat, freak," Derek instructed. "We're going to be busy the rest of the night. Oh, and leave the booze on your way out. Appreciate you hooking us up."

I left the bottle he requested. Shattered against the wall.

And as I walked away, I vowed no woman would ever capture my heart again.

"You're awfully quiet over there," Delaney says, pulling me from the past. "Thank you for bringing me with you. Oh, turn here, that's the entrance we use to get to our place."

I follow her directions and we're soon pulling into a parking spot. Once I park, I get out and help her down since Hammer's truck is jacked up and she's so short, I'm afraid she'll hurt herself trying to jump down. When she unlocks their door, I place my hand on her arm and state, "Let me check it out first, okay?"

Pulling my gun from its holster at my back, I carefully check out their apartment. Assured that all is okay, I hurry to the door and motion her inside. She smiles and states, "Help yourself to something to drink. I won't take too long, but I definitely want to clean myself up and change out of my horrorfest outfit."

I smirk at her because as far as I'm concerned, outside of the dried blood on her shirt and the bruises now covering her face and arms, she looks fine. But chicks are strange and feel they have to be ready to stroll down a runway or some shit, so I settle on the couch and grab the remote. "Take your time."

After finding a mindless show on, I scroll through my phone while I wait. A blood-curdling scream has me on my feet, gun in hand while rushing into the bathroom to see Delaney, wet from a shower, standing naked on the toilet lid.

"S-s-s-pider," she shakily says, pointing toward the corner of the shower.

Turning to see this spider and confident it'll end up being no bigger than a pinhead, I nearly screech myself when I see the biggest, hairiest motherfucking spider sitting up in the corner.

"Jesus, fuck, damn," I sputter, "what the fuck is that thing?"

"I-I-think it's our neighbor's pet."

"Pets wear leashes, collars, stupid sparkly shit, hell, they even wear costumes and clothes these days. They don't have eight legs, a shit ton of eyes, or fangs," I retort, grabbing her and making a run for it.

Do I notice she fits in my arms as though she's made for me?

Yes, yes, I do.

Do I stop and consider the ramifications for what I'm considering?

No, no I do not.

CHAPTER ELEVEN

Delaney

I had everything together for Honor when I decided to take a quick shower. This morning's 'adventure' with the deer then sitting for hours in blood-crusted clothing had me feeling icky. Seeing Bart's 'pet' staring at me gave me a heart attack and now I find myself in my room, held in the very capable arms of Glacier.

My heart is pounding as I look at him, until I see the pulse in his neck pounding, and realize he's likely feeling the same or similar emotions. "I'm too heavy, you should put me down," I tell him, very aware of the fact that I'm naked, my nipples are distended since I'm pressed against his chest, and there's a throbbing between my legs that has me blushing.

"You're not too heavy, but I will so you can get dressed."

Disappointment wars inside when after he puts me down, he steps back from me and heads to the door.

"You don't have to leave," I whisper, unsure where my bravery is coming from. I know I have a sassy side, but when it comes to something I promised I would wait to give away, the fact I'm considering it with someone I literally just met a few hours earlier is shocking to me.

Turning back to face me, he says, "As much as I want to, and believe me, I definitely do, you're not the kind of woman who deserves to be fucked and tossed aside, and I can't promise anything beyond that, Delaney. You heard me earlier. I'm a freak, a weirdo. I have sensory issues, I like things a certain way, and I fixate on shit that interests me. You can do far better."

"Did I say I wanted the white picket fence and a ring? No, I didn't. How do you know I would want more than to scratch an itch?"

You know you do, my brain whispers.

"Because looking around your room, I see someone who has created a sanctuary of sorts. All of this," he replies, waving his hand around, "reflects who you are, and that's not a hangaround or a club girl. You're ol' lady material, and I've never wanted one of those."

As he speaks, I watch his mannerisms and body language. I can see he's physically attracted to me if the bulge in his pants is any indication. I also note that while he's saying one thing, his expression is a mixture of hope and fear. He *does* want more than just a casual fuck, but someone or something has hurt him in the past and he doesn't think he deserves more.

Sighing, I nod. "We don't really have time now, anyhow, but I'd like the opportunity to revisit this once I'm sure Honor is going to be okay."

"Get dressed, pixie. I'll be waiting. Oh, and definitely call your neighbor about that fucker in the bathroom, or I'll shoot it."

I can't help my giggles as I pull out some clean clothes and quickly dress. Braiding my hair, I make sure I've got everything I need before I snag the bag I dropped in front of Honor's door and head back into the living room. Once we're back in Hammer's truck on the way to the hospital, I text Bart, who sends back a bunch of laughing emojis.

The asshole.

"Oh, Honor," I cry, tears pouring down my face as I look down at her small form in the hospital bed. "I'm so sorry I didn't know sooner what was happening."

She doesn't answer, as she was sedated while they examined her then worked to clean her up and take care of her injuries. Yet, I know she's in a bad way, and guilt courses through me. If I hadn't fallen asleep while grading papers, would I have seen the app sooner? Could I have prevented this somehow?

Glacier's arm wraps around my shoulder and I feel a soft kiss against my temple. "Pixie, why don't you run and grab us something to eat?" he quietly asks. "Looks like we're going to be here for a while."

"Okay. But just to say, hospital food sucks."

"I'll call into the diner and order us some specials," Gunner replies. "That work?"

"Okay," I murmur, my eyes never leaving my best friend's bruised and battered face.

I see a flash of green and realize Glacier's handing me some money. "I can pay for it," I protest.

His brow raises as he shakes his head. "I'm paying. Don't worry about getting drinks, saw a vending machine on our way up here."

"Okay. I'll be back shortly."

CHAPTER TWELVE

Glacier

With Delaney gone to pick up the food, it's just me, Gunner, and Savage, watching Honor as she sleeps while we wait for her to wake up.

Her list of physical injuries is rather extensive; a broken arm, several cracked ribs, lacerations that required stitches, bruises all over, a concussion, and trauma to her genital area. She's on mega doses of antibiotics, they've given her something to combat against sexually transmitted illnesses as well as pregnancy, and her arm has been casted. If the situation wasn't so fucked up, I'd smile because it's purple, her favorite color. Well, it was when we were kids, anyhow. She may have grown out of it for all I know. Still, seeing her lying so still, so broken, has me equal parts angry and upset.

No woman should ever be brutalized in any fashion, and from the little I've gleaned from Gunner and his brothers, what they did to Honor is typical behavior for them. Men like that aren't even men in my book; they're fucking sickos. Hell, most of society thinks I'm a freak and strange, but I'd never in a million years even consider treating a woman so horribly.

I know the minute she wakes up and realizes she's not alone, but don't I say anything, just observe, which is my norm. When I see the tears flowing freely down her face, my heart clenches. We might have rescued her but while the physical injuries will heal, I'm worried about the mental damage that may remain.

"What are you doing here?" she asks, finally looking at me. She doesn't maintain eye contact for long; just glances at me then looks over my shoulder. She's holding herself taut, and I don't know if it's from the pain she's undoubtedly in, or she's trying to keep the memories at bay.

"Came to see you," I reply. I don't remind her that she knew I was coming up to South Carolina and had planned to take her and her roommate out to dinner.

"When do you go back?" she asks, her tone sounding almost desperate.

"Depends." I shrug before glancing at the other two men in the room before looking back at Honor. I don't want to leave before I know she's going to be okay, but I also know I can't stay up here forever; I've got a job and responsibilities to my club and brothers. "Why?"

"Can I come live with you?" she blurts out, a sob falling free.

I know she's hurting but seeing the devastation on Gunner's and Savage's face has me hesitating. But it was her and I against the world for years until we were free from the system, and I promised her as kids I'd always have her back.

"Honor," Gunner rasps out.

I look at the other two men in the room before bringing my gaze back to her. "If that's what you need right now, then yeah, you can come back with me," I reply. "Whatever you have to have, Honor, you just have to ask."

CHAPTER THIRTEEN

Delaney

As I approach the door with bags of food in my arms, I hear Honor asking Glacier if she can come live with him. "Not without me, heifer!" I declare, practically dropping the bags inside the door and rushing to her side.

"What do you mean, not without you?" she asks me.

"I'm not about to lose my best friend. If you go, I'm going with you."

Before she can respond, Dr. Michaels walks in and the air in the room changes. "It's good to see you awake. How are you feeling?" she asks Honor.

"I feel like I've been hit by a Mack truck several times."

"I'm sure that's a good way to explain it all things considering," Dr. Michaels replies, before looking at the rest of us. "Would you all mind stepping out for a moment so I may have a word in private with my patient?"

While none of us want to leave, if the tension in the room is any indication, eventually, the four of us are in the hallway with the door closed. As I wait for the doctor to finish with Honor, I start thinking about everything I'm going to have to do in order to go with her. It might mean my job, but because of the varying certifications I've added to my degree, I'm pretty sure I can substitute teach at least. I know I can take a leave of absence and use the sick and vacation time I've accumulated to cover me financially. Plus, even though I'm no longer in contact with my family, I *did* receive an inheritance from my maternal grandparents that's just been collecting interest.

The bottom line is, I'm going. I'm sure a psychologist would tell me my guilt over the situation is driving my decision, but it's more than that. Honor saved me in so many ways I can't *not* be there to help her through this nightmare she's experiencing. Because she only had one night with Savage, so while she's no longer a virgin, she was raped and that's going to fuck with her head.

By the time the doctor leaves, I have a list running in my head of everything I need to take care of before we can go.

It takes a week for me to pack up the things we'll need in Georgia, which works out since Honor developed a fever from an infection, so she ended up being in the hospital a few days longer than originally planned. We'll have connecting suites at their clubhouse, which is an old boarding school, so I'll be available to check on her. As I lug a cooler full of drinks down to my car, Asa is suddenly there taking it from me.

"I've got it, where do you want me to put it?" he asks.

Since my car was totaled because of the deer, I'm currently driving a rental car while my insurance company works on getting me a value. Once I'm in Georgia, I plan to turn the rental car in as Asa said there are plenty of vehicles I can borrow while I'm there. Right now, I'm driving a mid-size SUV, which I kind of like, because the seats go down, giving me more room.

"Can you put it in the middle behind the driver and passenger seats? That way, Honor can reach back and grab our drinks without any problem," I reply.

"Definitely."

Without another word, he walks away, so I go through our apartment one more time to make sure I've got everything we could possibly need. Gunner's ol' lady came by with some of the other women and they took all our perishable items back to the clubhouse. The non-perishable foods are going to be donated to the local food bank, since we don't know how long we'll be gone. Gunner told Honor he would cover our rent while we're gone, so that's one less worry. I mean, we argued with him about it, but he told us both, in no uncertain terms, that it was the least he could do considering the circumstances.

Honor still isn't talking all that much, which I hope changes once she feels safe again. Although, I'm not sure she ever truly will, especially since what happened occurred at her job. Still, the hospital has been good to her as well. She's on an extended leave of absence, and because it happened on hospital grounds, Human Resources did something so she's still going to get a paycheck, and her insurance will continue as well.

My job was understanding as well. Hopefully, I can find a substitute position while I'm in Georgia, but it really depends on Honor and how she's doing. She's my priority right now, even though the more I'm around Asa, the more I'm glad we'll be around him all the time. Apparently, he lives in the clubhouse as well, so I'm hoping that we can get to know each other a little better.

Time will tell, I guess. Walking over to where Honor is just sitting on the couch staring into space, I clear my throat then ask, "Are you ready, wench?"

Despite the fact I announced my presence, she still jumps, and I feel guilt flow through me once again. What am I talking about? It's been there constantly since this whole thing happened. Each pump of my heart makes me wonder what I could've done differently. Every cry she makes in the middle of the night that has me rushing to her side causes me to curse the fact I fell asleep that fateful evening.

She smiles at me, but it doesn't come close to reaching her eyes, which are dead looking, and nods. "Just have to get my purse. Asa already carried my other things down to the car."

Trying to make her smile, I state, "Maybe we'll actually be able to stop at Buc-ee's!"

"That would be nice." Her voice is flat; no emotion can be heard at all.

"Well, I'm gonna pee really quick then I'll be ready," I tell her before I walk toward the bathroom.

Once inside, I silently cry for my best friend. I don't know how to reach her, what to do so she knows that inside where it counts, she's still the same person she always was, that nothing those bastards did to her was on her at all. Yet, when I tell her we'll find a counselor, I'll be happy to go with her, we'll do whatever it takes so she can heal, she merely nods.

After finishing, I scrub my face to wash the evidence of my tears away, although if I'm being truthful, she won't notice. Not because she's selfish since she's the most giving, kind, loving person I know, but because of the fact she's so withdrawn, she's unobservant right now.

I gather my own purse and look round one last time, seeing that Honor is apparently already down at the car. With a small sigh, I open the door, walk through then lock it behind me. I'm grateful that Gunner will keep an eye on our place; we've made it into a homey sanctuary, and I want it to stay the same until we're back under its roof once again.

As I reach my car and maneuver to the driver's side, I see Asa glance up from where he was leaning on the passenger side window talking to Honor. His brows furrow, he hits the window then practically stalks to where I'm standing.

Despite his harsh movements, his hand is gentle when it cups my chin, and he lifts my face so he can look at me. "What's wrong, Pixie?" he growls out. "Why were you crying?" He keeps his voice low so Honor doesn't overhear; but again, she's so lost in her own little world, she doesn't notice.

"It's nothing, Asa. Just got overwhelmed for a few minutes is all. What if we can't reach her? She's so closed off, it's scary."

"We'll break through, I promise," he asserts. "Patsy, Atlas' ol' lady, has been where she is now and thanks to a great therapist, plus Atlas and her service dog, she's managed to find healing. I'm sure it still bothers her, but she's got a good support system, and so does Honor. We'll be there for her, and I know when she's ready, her brother will be as well."

"What about Savage?" I ask. "He seemed torn up by what happened."

"I suspect that brother has been kicking his own ass ever since we found out she was taken. The thing is, even if she *had* been with him, that's no guarantee that those fuckers woulda left her alone from what I was able to understand. Seems they're related to Avery and do whatever they can to fuck with her peace or some shit."

"Barbaric assholes."

"You got that right, babe. Now, let's hit the road. I thought we'd stop at Buc-ee's, see if that gets any kind of reaction outta her."

I grin because I've never been to one yet, and I'm excited to see the convenience store on steroids that everyone seems overwhelmed by. "Right behind you."

"Yeah, about that. Poseidon and Trident will be in front of me, then you'll be behind me, with Atlas and Brooks at the rear of our little caravan."

"Oh, okay. Why? Are we in danger?" I question, glancing around.

"No, not really. They just want to make sure we're covered."

I shrug, not really understanding their ways as he opens my car door for me. "Thanks, Asa."

"Not a problem, Pixie."

CHAPTER FOURTEEN

Glacier

Surprisingly, despite all the extra people we have in our little caravan, the trip is relatively smooth. We stopped about two hours into the trip for something to eat and to stretch, and I got to see a little more of how Delaney is around others. She asked the brothers about their ol' ladies and kids, as well as about the club businesses, and seemed genuinely interested.

We're now back on the road and Poseidon has signaled that he's turning onto the ramp to take us to Buc-ee's. I hope this'll break through Honor's wall; she was present at breakfast, but not really. Even Delaney's reminder to check her pump was met with a blank stare. Part of me wishes I could just shake her and pull her out of this shit, but another part recognizes that she's broken, shattered into a million pieces.

I just hope we have the glue needed to put her back together again. Failing is not an option; Honor saved my ass so many times when we were kids, I owe it to her to give it my best shot. I just worry because I'm not good with words as a rule. Of course, Honor knows how I am so there's that to consider as well.

Delaney is turning into a beautiful distraction for me. I'm definitely intrigued and wish I were different so I could pursue something with her, but then I think of my high school shame and realize I know nothing about relationships.

As I pull over to the pumps, I see everyone else doing the same. Getting out, I start filling the truck, then walk over to Delaney's car. "Go inside, I got this," I tell her.

"Are you sure? I've been pumping my own gas for a long time now," she replies.

"As long as I'm around, you don't have to do that," I state. "Now, you and Honor go indulge your love for all things Buc-ee," I tease.

Which shocks the shit out of me. I don't tease. I don't joke. I keep things simple and to the point. But for her, I'm willing to try. When she grins at me, pulls her purse from the car and manages to get Honor out as well, I smirk at her.

———⋲

Our short trip to Buc-ee's added nearly an hour onto our trip because they got lost in the merchandise section. By lost, I mean that by the time we went inside, hit the head, then started looking for them, they had two carts overflowing with beaver items. While Atlas laughed his ass off, Trident added to it with things for his girls, which then had Poseidon, Brooks, and Atlas looking around as well.

Sighing, I can't help the chuckle that escapes when I think about how full the back of the box truck now is, considering that at the checkout, there was a brief discussion about what belonged to who until Poseidon finally tossed his credit card down and paid for all of it, despite Delaney's protests.

She doesn't realize it yet, but when she's with any one of us, she won't pay a damn thing. Ever. And it's not because we're a bunch of cavemen who think a woman is beneath us; it's one of the many ways we show them we care.

I yawn loudly as the road moves beneath me, knowing I'll be sore when we finally get home. The box truck is comfortable enough for a cage, I guess, but the suspension isn't as good as my girl's is, so my ass has felt every bounce and dip in the road.

"Just a little further, Glace, you got this," I mutter to myself, as I see Poseidon signal for our exit. I'm eager to reach the clubhouse, get the prospects to unload the girls' shit, then hit my shower before I crash on my bed. Ever since Honor was taken, the stress has been ever-present, and while I know we've got a long way to go where she's concerned, I feel as though we're in the home stretch.

If only I had known how wrong I was.

CHAPTER FIFTEEN

Delaney

"Honor, I got Dr. Williams' number from Patsy," I say, walking into her bedroom.

We've been here a month and yesterday, Patsy and Roane caught her right after she had taken a bunch of pills in an attempt to overdose. Thankfully, Trident was able to reverse it all, and after a night spent puking her guts out, he deemed she was out of the woods.

However, she promised she'd start seeing a counselor after I threatened to call Gunner. To make sure she does, Asa and I plan to alternate taking her and picking her up. Hopefully, the counselor, who Patsy highly recommends, can break through because nothing any one of us has said to her has made the slightest impact at all.

"Okay, thanks," she murmurs, not quite meeting my eyes.

"Want me to call for you?" I ask.

"No, I'll do it," she replies, holding her hand out for the slip of paper I wrote the number on.

"Okay, let me know when your appointment is, and I'll take you."

"Thanks, Delaney," she whispers.

"You're welcome, Honor."

I walk back into my room, the guilt still hanging around me like a shroud. I missed those signs as well. I mean, she kept the drinking somewhat hidden, only having one or two when we were hanging out downstairs in the common area. What I didn't know was she had gotten her hands on several bottles since the bar is easily accessible, and she was drinking herself into a stupor most nights.

Those were the ones I didn't wake up to her screaming, lost in the thralls of a nightmare. Stupid me thought she was coming to terms with shit, but how could she when she refused to talk to anyone about what happened? She'd spend hours in the bathroom, scrubbing herself until she was nearly raw, until I threatened to stay in there with her, so she didn't hurt herself.

Most nights, though, I end up in her bed, holding her as she cries, which breaks my heart into a million pieces. While I mull over how I can help her, I finish getting dressed so I can head down for breakfast.

Walking into the kitchen, I hear Roane ask, "Are you going to see Dr. Williams today?"

"Yes, it's this afternoon," Honor says, taking a sip of her coffee.

"That's good." This comes from Patsy. "Is Delaney taking you?"

"Yes, I am," I reply, walking over to the refrigerator to grab a cold diet soda. She was obviously able to get in to see the counselor today, which is great news because I'm at my wits end at this point, and I feel as though Asa is too.

We sit and eat breakfast; the conversation light and I marvel over the women who make up this club. They're all kind and loving, with backbones of steel. Perfect matches for the men, that's for damn sure! My mind meanders to Asa and how his presence affects me. I've tried to let him know I'd like to revisit the discussion we started well over a month ago, but he shies away from it and even me.

"You're awfully quiet, Delaney, you okay?" Patsy questions.

"Just thinking is all," I reply. "Nothing earth-shattering."

"It's Glacier, isn't it?" Roane asks.

"What? What do you mean?"

"We've noticed how he watches you when he thinks no one is paying any attention to him," Patsy advises. "He's got it bad, girl."

"No, he doesn't," I protest. "If he did, he wouldn't avoid me the way he does."

"I think, and this is just me, of course, that something happened to him when he was younger," Patsy says. "He probably thinks he's not good enough or some shit like that."

"Something did," Honor whispers, shocking the three of us. She usually doesn't engage unless she's spoken to directly, so her breaking into the conversation is hopefully a good sign.

"It did?" I reply, my heart breaking for a younger Asa. I know he's developed some great coping abilities to deal with his autism so others don't notice, but I suspect when he was younger that he wasn't as adept.

"Some bitch used him, played up to him like she was head over heels for him, only to break him when he showed up and she was in the hotel room fucking her so-called ex," Honor bitterly retorts. "He wouldn't let me beat her ass, either, the fucking twat."

"So, he's never been in another relationship?" I ask.

"Nope," she replies, popping the 'p' like a teenager. I shake my head because she knows it drives me nuts, but seeing some 'normal' behaviors from her has me internally smiling. Maybe Honor's coming back to us after all. "He just fucks and dumps. I was hoping that him meeting you would change that, but I guess it hasn't."

"Oh, I think he's noticed her," Patsy teases. "He's just not sure he's good enough, or whatever bullshit excuse he's got running through his mind. It'll be up to you to make the first moves, Delaney."

"Me?" I squeak out. "You're talking to a card-carrying virgin here! I have no clue how to make a move on someone."

Now I'm morosely studying my hands as Patsy and Roane offer up ideas for me to make Asa realize I'd like a shot with him. Half of their suggestions are so crazy, I'd never have the guts. Finally, I put my hand up.

"What on earth? Why are you raising your hand?" Roane asks.

"So I can get a word in edgewise?" I retort. "Listen, when Honor was um… in the hospital, he took me back by our apartment so I could get some clothes and such for her. Anyhow, I was covered in blood from my airbags after hitting a deer, so once I had her stuff packed, I jumped into the shower only to realize that my neighbor's pet tarantula had somehow gotten loose and into our apartment because he was up in the corner of the stall, staring at me. I screamed, Asa came in with his gun in his hands looking for the threat, then when he realized I wasn't talking about a teensy tiny one, he grabbed me up and carried me to my room. Y'all, I was *naked* and when I let him know I was interested, he gave me a whole song and dance about why it wouldn't be a good idea. I told him we'd revisit the discussion, because I thought I was getting the vibe that he was interested. Only, he hasn't been alone around me since we got here. I think y'all are wrong, he's not interested, so it's better not to pursue something that'll go nowhere fast. Plus, that's not why I'm here."

"You're still allowed to have a life," Honor quietly says.

"I have a life, Honor, and right now, my focus is helping you heal," I reply.

"You can do both, Dee," she insists.

"Actually, it makes no sense to start something when we live in South Carolina," I tell her. "I don't want to do a long-distance relationship, Honor. I want to be able to call or send a text at the spur of the moment for us to meet up for lunch or dinner, that kind of thing. An eight hour plus drive isn't conducive to spontaneity."

My heart sinks because being totally honest with myself, Asa's the first man I've ever met that would make me consider something so extreme. Why he won't discuss what happened in the apartment with me is beyond my understanding. I just know when he's nearby, my heart rate accelerates, my palms get sweaty, and my panties dampen almost uncomfortably. Not that I share that information with my bestie and the ol' ladies. Nope, my lips are definitely remaining sealed on this one.

"Well, anything can happen, and we *do* have schools here," Patsy chimes in. "Now, what time is your appointment?"

"It's at one o'clock," Honor says.

Glancing at my phone, I see we have a few hours before we have to leave. "Then I'm going to do some laundry and make sure my resume prints correctly." At Honor's look I continue. "I'm going to drop it off at the elementary school so I can be considered for substitute teaching."

"Oh, that's good," she says. Again, no real emotion in her voice and her face is devoid of a smile.

"Yeah, I figured it would keep me busy when you're doing therapy."

"Plus, there's enough of us to get you back and forth, Honor, if she's called in to substitute," Roane adds.

"Meet you out front in an hour?" I ask as I pull up in front of a low, nicely landscaped brick building that looks more like a house than a doctor's office. Glacier is following behind me on his bike, giving us privacy, I guess. Or maybe he doesn't want to be alone with me. Who knows?

"Yeah, I'll just sit right over there on that bench," she says, pointing to where there's a bench beneath two trees.

"Okay. Maybe after, if you feel like it, we can grab something to eat? We haven't done that in a while."

"Sounds good to me. Thanks, Dee, for bringing me."

"Anytime, wench. You should know that by now."

Her voice is barely above a whisper as she gets out of my car, but I still hear her when she says, "I do."

Glacier's at my window by the time she walks through the door. "I'll follow you over to the school. Did you ask her about getting something to eat?"

I nod, my voice temporarily gone when his scent wafts through my senses. If I could bottle it, I'd be a rich woman; it's clean yet earthy, and makes me want to push my face into his neck and breathe deeply. "She said that sounded good."

He runs his hand across his face. "I hope this works. She doesn't seem to be getting any better and it gets harder every week to hold Savage and Gunner back."

"I can only imagine. They're both rather… intense," I tease.

"Not to me, and I totally get it because if I was in their situation, I'd want to be with my woman, not hundreds of miles away, waiting and worrying."

"Well, they are to me and you're right, I don't think she is getting better. She doesn't really speak unless spoken to, and her nightmares are getting worse. I thought she'd start to open up more being here with you, but she hasn't, Asa. I'm not sure what to do!"

"We hope that therapy does the trick, and continue to be by her side until she's ready to talk."

Sighing, I nod. "I guess you're right. Okay, I need to run to the school, but you don't have to follow me. I'm sure you've got things to do."

"I do later but not right now. You got the address in your GPS?" At my nod, he taps my door and turns. "I'll follow you."

A man of few words. I find I like it more and more each passing day. Now to get him to grasp that fact.

CHAPTER SIXTEEN

Glacier

As I follow Delaney and Honor after she picked her up from the therapist's office, my mind wanders to Honor and my last conversation with her brother, Gunner. In typical fashion, he insisted he and Savage come down to collect her and I had to tell him she wasn't ready. I didn't spill the beans about her trying to kill herself by overdosing. I promised I wouldn't, and I won't, but if she tries something like that again, all bets will be off. Like Delaney said, she seems to grow more and more withdrawn each and every day. Even with Patsy and Roane insinuating themselves into her life, she says and does the bare minimum.

That's not Honor, but since I'm not a chick and haven't gone through what she did, I don't know if her actions are normal or not. I just know that everything I've tried so far has fallen short, and I'm at a loss about what to try next. As safe as she is within the walls of our property, especially the clubhouse, she's always jumping at every single sound. A glimmer of an idea emerges, and I decide to discuss it with Delaney when we have a moment alone.

I snort out loud; since that time in her apartment when I walked away with my dick as hard as a steel pike, I haven't allowed myself to be by myself with her. Why? Because despite my overwhelming fear concerning relationships, with her I want to try.

Which is absolutely insane since she's only here temporarily. How on earth can we build something with each other when she's eventually going to go home to South Carolina? It's not like I'm going to switch clubs, although I suspect Gunner would sponsor me.

When Delaney signals to pull into the diner, I slow down and follow behind her, eager to hear with my own ears how Honor's session went. I've told her I'm willing to go in with her if she wants; whatever it takes, I'll be there for her. Poseidon understands and so does Atlas, which is good, because we're suddenly getting a shit ton of custom helmet orders. Thankfully, we tell prospective customers that there is no rushing the process and to expect at least a six-to-eight-week turnaround once the order has been processed and the design approved.

As I make my way back to my area of the shop, my mind is whirling with some of the things Honor shared over lunch. Other than saying the therapist will see her twice a week to start, she said a whole lot of nothing.

And that's concerning to me, because even though she's been quieter since the assault, she's always had something to say. But the blankness in her eyes, her overall lackluster appearance, and the way she won't meet anyone's gaze has me worried she's going to try to check out again.

What if she tries and no one's around this time to save her? Worse yet, what if she *is* saved but causes herself irreparable injury and ends up spending the rest of her life in a vegetative state?

Part of me thinks I should call Gunner and fill him in, yet I can't bring myself to do it. It feels like I'd be betraying Honor by doing so, and I'm positive that between me, Delaney, my brothers and their ol' ladies, as well as Dr. Williams, we can break through to her. Make her understand that what happened, while terrible, doesn't define who she is as a person, nor should it impact any future relationships she might have.

Hell, as angry as Savage was about what happened, he wasn't put off by her becoming his ol' lady even though she had been gang raped. He was more upset about the fact that someone dared to harm a woman who was under the protection of the DRMC than anything. Because while she's not his ol' lady at this point, she *is* Gunner's sister and as such, should be off limits. However, from what I was able to gather, Avery's siblings have no honor whatsoever and are willing to harm anyone they can, regardless of whether or not they're women or children.

Sighing, I open up my laptop and pull down the first order. Thirty minutes later, I've got the design traced and am working on painting the outline when I hear footsteps coming up behind me. Because of my issues, I know whoever is there is walking louder than normal so I'll know they're coming. Putting down the brush, I turn on my chair to see Atlas, his dog by his side.

"What's up, Brother?" I ask, grateful for the break.

I tend to get so involved in what I'm doing that I forget to eat or drink, so his interruption is welcome.

"How did today go?" he asks.

I look at him and shrug. "Not really sure, Brother. She shared a lot of nothing when we stopped to eat after her appointment. Part of me wonders if she even went, y'know? Except I saw her walk into the building before me and Delaney pulled away."

"I had a thought," he says. At my look, he sneers then retorts, "Okay, okay, it was *Patsy* who had the idea. Since you made it clear that Honor has Type 1 diabetes so that the prospects cook well-rounded meals for her, she started checking into something. What do you think about me reaching out to Nick to see if he's got a dog that could help her with that? Maybe one who can also be trained for protection? Ridley has really helped Patsy with her PTSD, so if he was able to combine the two, it might help her brother loosen the reins."

I burst into laughter as I think about Gunner and how overprotective he is when it comes to Honor. I suspect after what happened, his solution will be to wrap her in cotton wool then stick her somewhere that she'll have constant supervision, something she'll hate with a passion.

"That could work. Do you think it's possible, though? I'll pay for it, Brother," I reply.

"They only accept donations from clubs, Glace," he states.

"Then we better figure out what they need so I can send them a fucking tractor trailer full," I say, causing him to chuckle.

"We'll all want in on that. You know how we all feel about what happened to her."

I nod, because my brothers have gone out of their way to make sure they don't do anything to startle her or intimidate her. The ol' ladies have taken both her and Delaney under their wings as well. Most afternoons, they manage to get her down to the inside pool and I've seen her smile a few times at the kids' antics, especially Noah.

"Yeah, I do. I appreciate all that everyone's done for both of them."

"It's what we do. They're family, Glacier. May not all be part of this club, but we take care of those who we love," he says. "Alright, I'll reach out. May take some time, because knowing Nick, he'll search for the absolute best dog for her."

"Works for me. Don't think we're going anywhere for some time."

"At least until Savage and Gunner storm the proverbial gates."

CHAPTER SEVENTEEN

Delaney

"She's not doing much better," I murmur to Glacier as we watch Honor go into the therapist's building.

"No, I don't think so either. Come on, I'll take you to get some breakfast before I head into work. You're okay to pick her up, right?"

"Yeah, I think we're just going to go shopping. I got a call yesterday afternoon and will be taking over for the elementary school's special ed teacher for the rest of the year since she's going out on maternity leave."

"That's great news, Pixie," he says, grinning at me. "Okay, I'll follow you. Diner okay?"

"Works for me, Asa. Thank you."

"Do you think this will work?" I ask Honor as she stands beside me. "I mean, they're elementary school kids, but it's a lot warmer here than at home."

"It's fine, Dee."

I'm trying to be understanding, but it's as though I'm talking to a mannequin for all the emotion I see and hear. Frustrated tears come to my eyes; I'm scared for my best friend. She's lost weight, her hair is listless and dull, and she's almost robotic in everything she does nowadays. I don't know how to reach her and worry that if a breakthrough of some sort doesn't happen soon, she's going to be lost to all of us.

Taking a deep breath, I will away my tears then gather the clothes I set to the side. "Come on, let's check out and head back to the clubhouse. I have some paperwork to sign online, and I'm sure you're ready for a rest after therapy."

"Yeah, I think I'll take a bath then a nap."

"Honor, what do you think…"

Instead of finishing my thoughts, I scream for Glacier as I rush to the bathtub where Honor is passed out, blood dripping from her wrists. "No, no, no, this isn't happening," I scream, as I grab two towels, wrap each wrist up and use a hair tie from my own hair to keep them closed. "Don't leave me, Honor, don't you fucking dare leave me! I can't do this without you!"

I don't know how to put more pressure on both wrists at the same time, but as I'm about to crawl into the tub with her and lay on one while holding the other, Asa bursts into the room. He figures out what's going on at a glance and he scoops her up, uncaring that she's naked, and rushes from the room, my makeshift bandages holding steady.

"Grab my phone, scroll to Trident and call him to let him know we're bringing her in," he grunts out, running down the stairs.

Somehow, I manage to snag it out of his back pocket, and quickly make the call. As we enter the common room, I see a tablecloth and pull it off the table to wrap around her body. One of the prospects sees us running and opens the door then quickly gets the club SUV unlocked, before jumping into the driver's seat. Asa and I slide into the back, both of us now able to apply pressure to the wounds which are still seeping blood.

"She's so pale," I whisper, my throat raw from screaming. "Honor, honey, please wake up," I cry, tears still freely flowing down my face.

"Honor, dammit, this ain't the way," Asa growls out, his face pale and taut with fear. "Not on my watch, squirt. Not on my fucking watch!"

A trip that usually takes about twenty minutes takes half of that, and I see Trident along with a team of doctors standing at the emergency room doors with a gurney. Honor's quickly transferred from the SUV to the gurney then whisked away, leaving the three of us alone.

"I'll go park the car," the prospect says, leaving me with Asa who quickly pulls me into his arms.

Before I can say or do anything, he's kissing me, something I never expected or anticipated. Giving in to the sensations coursing through me, I relax into his embrace and kiss him back, our tongues dueling as we learn about each other. For what feels like hours, but is in reality only seconds, I lose myself in all that he is; strong, loyal, loving, kind. As he pulls back slightly, both of us breathing hard, he lightly kisses my lips again.

"Thank you for finding her," he rasps out, his thumbs caressing my cheeks. "I hope… I hope we were in time."

"Me too," I reply, my voice faint as the pain in my throat keeps me from speaking any louder. "Let's go in and find out where we need to wait."

As we sit in the waiting room, my hand firmly clenched in his, it slowly fills up with his brothers and their ol' ladies. Patsy and Atlas thankfully brought both of us clean clothes since we were both covered in her blood, and I was wet from the tub.

I'm lost in my thoughts, worried about Honor, when I hear Asa mutter, "Shoulda fucking gone with my gut."

"What do you mean?"

When I couldn't speak above a whisper, Asa insisted I get checked out. Trident worked his magic and within no time at all, I was being examined. The official diagnosis is laryngitis so I shouldn't be talking, but I have to know what he means. If nothing else, it's pulling me away from my own thoughts which have the horror scene I walked in on running over in a continuous loop.

"I knew something was off with her. I shoulda pressed her, made her talk."

"If she wasn't ready to talk, she wasn't going to do anything but give you lip service," Patsy interjects.

Asa nods as though he agrees so I nudge him. "She's always been stubborn, Delaney, ever since we were kids. If she doesn't want to do something, she won't do it, and it's been like that even before her kidnapping and assault," he says. "But I know her signs and I shoulda pressed harder."

"Brother, don't take on that mantle of guilt," Atlas states. "She's deeply troubled, as I suspect anyone who's gone through what she did would be. The important thing now is to make sure she gets the help she so obviously needs."

"Then that's what we'll do," he advises. "I'll sit in on her therapy appointments if I have to, I can work after hours."

"We've got your back, Glacier," Poseidon promises. "Worst case scenario, we'll get Loki and Kaya in to paint the helmets so they look good, then we can do the rest of the process."

Tears fill my eyes at how his brothers are stepping up and stepping in to help so he can focus on Honor's recovery. He must notice because he squeezes my hand, causing me to look at him. "It's going to be fine," he asserts. "We're going to make it be that way."

Hours later, a doctor walks into the room and looks around, his eyes widening almost comically at the sheer number of people. "I take it all of you are here for Honor?" he asks. I can see the exhaustion on his face, as well as the evidence of what he was doing on his scrubs.

Asa stands and pulls me up alongside him as he approaches the doctor. "I'm her cousin," he says, holding out his hand. The doctor doesn't even hesitate, he takes Asa's hand and grips it firmly before letting it go.

"Not going to lie to you folks, it was touch and go there for a time. However, whoever wrapped her wrists and put the hair ties around them, you gave her a fighting chance. She's had two transfusions already, and we've surgically repaired the damage she caused. They're moving her up to ICU so we can observe her for possible infection, and due to the circumstances, she's been placed on a psych hold."

"What does that mean?" Asa asks, his brow furrowed.

"She won't be released until we're sure she's no longer a danger to herself," the doctor replies. "While it's past visiting hours, I can take you up to at least put your eyes on her."

"She's coming too," Asa states. "She's her best friend and the one who found her."

"That's fine. You did a good job, young lady."

Since I'm to refrain from talking according to the ER doctor who saw me earlier, I nod. I don't feel like I did a good job; if I had, maybe I would've seen the signs earlier too. Asa's not the only one who holds so much guilt over the whole situation. I carry my fair share.

CHAPTER EIGHTEEN

Glacier

After we peek in on Honor, who they've got heavily sedated right now, we head back to the waiting room to see Poseidon and Atlas waiting. "Figured we'd walk down with y'all," Poseidon says when he sees us. "Everyone else has headed back."

Only… they hadn't. When we got outside, we found a prospect there with another club vehicle, since the one we came in was covered in blood, along with the brothers waiting on their bikes.

Family.

My family.

Waiting for me so we can go home together. Squeezing Delaney's hand, unwilling to let her go, I help her into the SUV then slide in next to her. Once we're both buckled, I take her hand in mine again. Right now, she's a captive audience since she's supposed to rest her throat and not talk.

"Glacier, I picked up Delaney's prescription while I was out," the prospect, whose name escapes me, says as we fall in behind the bikes. "Left it at the bar."

"Thank you," I reply. Turning to her, I see she's not crying any longer, which is good. I'm no good with tears; in fact, most emotions tend to elude me.

She smiles up at me and my mind goes back to the kiss we shared. I've been resisting getting involved with her, but ever since my lips touched hers, all I can see is a future with her by my side. I just hope I'm not setting myself up for another heartbreak, because I suspect it would kill me.

"I'm sure Kaya's granny has cooked, with Mary's help and probably Poseidon's mom as well," I tell her. "We'll eat then I can help you clean up the en suite."

There's no way I want her to face that on her own. It looked like a fucking crime scene, with blood everywhere, and Delaney's terror-filled screams still fill my head. I've never been more scared in my entire life. Hell, even back as a kid when my dad was beating me, I was more resigned than anything, as though I deserved his wrath and abuse.

She's shaking her head no, but I'm not budging on this one, not at all. "Yeah, I am, Pixie. You're not doing that shit by yourself, you hear me?"

She huffs out a sigh, looking annoyed but finally shrugs as if she's agreeing with me. I'm pretty sure if she could talk, she'd use the age-old phrase of 'fine, whatever' on me, which makes me grin.

By the time we're done eating, I can see the toll today has taken on her as she's barely got her eyes open. Standing, I take her hand in mine, all while ignoring the knowing looks from my brothers, and lead us upstairs. When she pulls toward her room, I shake my head.

"No, babe, you're exhausted. Tomorrow's another day, in fact, I'll see if one of the prospects will clean it for you."

The look of gratitude she gives me makes me feel like puffing out my chest. Other than Honor, I haven't cared what any woman thought about me in more years than I can remember. Well, except for the brothers' ol' ladies, anyhow.

I lead her to my room and once I've unlocked the door,

usher her inside. "Let me get you something you can change into," I tell her, heading into the bedroom. It doesn't take me long to grab a T-shirt and pair of shorts which I hand to her. "Help yourself to whatever you need, Delaney, I'll wait out here for you."

She nods before heading into the bathroom and closing the door behind her. Once she's inside, I let out the breath I'm holding before I find clothes I can change into since I was able to get cleaned up at the hospital while she still had dried blood in her hair where it dragged across Honor's body.

I grab each of us a bottle of water and place them on the nightstands, as well as the prescription the prospect picked up for her, before pulling the covers back and sitting against the headboard, the remote in my hand. As I scroll mindlessly, my mind wanders to Delaney; all the hours we've spent together since she came to St. Marys with Honor, and I can't help the smile that crosses my face.

She's the first person I've met who gets me, who can handle my need for solitude from time to time. We've hung out downstairs in the common area with her grading papers and me working on new designs, and seeing the genuine interest she's displayed when I show her what I've done further melts the ice encasing my heart.

Around Delaney, the negative voices that still rise up even all these years later are silent. It's as if my inner self knows she's good for me. I guess it's time I accept that fact myself. I have no clue how we'd work things out once she goes back home, but as Trident is fond of saying, that's Future Glacier's problem. Snickering, I find something on I think she'll enjoy, then when it dawns on me how long she's been in the bathroom, I grow alarmed.

She wouldn't do what Honor did, I tell myself as I knife up off the bed.

Knocking on the door, I call out, "Delaney? You okay, babe?"

Instead of hearing a response, I hear a faint sob, which has me opening the door. I see her curled up on the bottom of the shower stall, her arms wrapped around her knees as she rocks back and forth, crying.

"Shit, fuck," I whisper as I get into the stall. "Shhh, Pixie, it's just me, I've got you, I've got you," I murmur, pulling her into my arms, uncaring that I'm getting soaked.

Which in and of itself is a huge thing since sensory issues rule my life. If I like a shirt? It better not have a tag inside; even cutting them out doesn't work. Jeans? I wear them during the workday having finally found a brand that's not too stiff, but as soon as I'm 'in' for the night, I switch to a pair of basketball shorts or sweatpants depending on the time of the year.

"I-I-I was s-s-s-so scared," she stammers out, her arms clutching me tightly. "I-I-I thought she was dead!" she wails, her voice sounding worse the longer she talks.

"Shhh, Delaney, try not to talk, babe," I reply. "I was scared too, never been more scared in my fucking life," I admit. "Don't think I'll ever forget the sound of your screams."

"S-s-sorry," she whispers.

"No need to apologize, you needed help, sweetheart, and while I know that's not why you were screaming, you got what was needed and we got her to the hospital in time."

She nods, her tears still freely flowing as the water pounds down her naked body. One which my own body has definitely noticed, if the hardon I'm sporting is any indication.

"Let's get you cleaned up and into bed, okay? I brought your medicine up and got some water so you can take it. Now, turn around and I'll wash your hair. Sorry that it's not the fruity stuff you use, but it is good stuff because Honor buys it for me."

I hear her sniffly giggle and grin, gathering some shampoo in my hands before applying it to her head. A low moan has my dick leaking precum, as I work the lather through her curly tresses. God, she's fucking gorgeous and doesn't have a damn clue.

While I look forward to a time we can enjoy a shower together under entirely different circumstances, tonight I focus on getting her clean so I can get her warmed up and into bed. Once I'm confident I have all the shampoo rinsed out of her hair, I step back and say, "Go ahead and rinse, Pixie. I'll grab your towel."

She nods before stepping fully underneath the stream of water, a sigh filling the stall. I take one last look then turn, adjusting my dick as I step out. Chastising myself as I quickly strip out of my wet clothes, I grab a towel and tie it around my waist, then grab two for her. The water turns off and she steps out, her eyes catching mine as I hand her both towels. When she does the turban thing with one of them, I can't help chuckling.

"Not gonna lie, but I think women are taught how to do that with their hair as soon as they can walk," I state. "I'll let you get dressed, I need to put on some dry clothes myself."

I leave her in the bathroom, giggling as she dries off. By the time she emerges, I'm back in the bed, my back against the headboard, my legs under the covers. While I wasn't in the military like the majority of my brothers, I'm just as anal about my space. I may not have a lot, but what I have is good quality, and I take care of it, including making my bed every morning.

She gives me a shy smile as she slides into the bed. "Take your medicine, Delaney. It'll help your throat. Think it's got a mild painkiller in it which should make it feel better."

Nodding, she takes her medicine then curls up on her side facing me. Scooting down, I move closer until I can feel the heat coming from her body. Cupping her face with one hand, I lean in and kiss her forehead.

"I know you've wanted to revisit the conversation we had several weeks ago, and I've been putting it off. I want to apologize to you for that, Delaney. It's definitely not you, it's one hundred percent me." At her look, I continue. "It's no secret that because I'm on the spectrum, I have a lot of quirks." She shrugs, making me grin. "Yeah, well, picture me in high school, not fully understanding what autism was exactly because the state said I was too old to be tested. There Honor and I were, trying different things we'd researched or gotten from our foster family who also did their own searching, so that I'd 'fit in' and be able to function. I finally had a few friends, was doing well enough in my classes that I wasn't in danger of failing, and had the normal teenage hormones coursing through me."

"What happened?" she mouths, which makes me lean in to kiss her since she didn't actually speak.

"Good girl," I praise. "Well, like most high schools, you have the various cliques. The jocks, the queen bees, the nerds, the stoners. Bethany Jayne Northrup was the head of the queen bees. She had been dating the school quarterback since birth." At her wide eyes, I chuckle. "Okay, so maybe not that long, but for all of high school anyways. They broke up and she started paying attention to me, a few weeks before prom. Honor said she was up to something, but I wouldn't listen to her, happy as a pig in shit that a popular girl wanted something to do with *me*, you know?" She nods, so I carry on with my sad tale, telling her how I busted my ass to get the money together for a room based on Bethany's promises, that I had practically ostracized Honor because she wouldn't let up on her suspicions, all of it. When I get to the end, she's got tears in her eyes and looks angry.

"You okay, babe?" I question.

She shakes her head, a murderous look on her face. When she makes stabbing motions into her hand, I throw back my head and burst into laughter, pulling her close.

"You wanna hurt her, huh?"

"Mmhm."

"Nuh uh uh, no talking," I admonish. "Trust me, Delaney, she ended up with the short end of the stick in the long run. Wanna know what happened?" She grins while nodding, so I continue once again. "Turns out while she was leading me on through the ring she had in my nose, her boyfriend was screwing everything that he could. He ended up giving her a few things, a baby as well as a sexually transmitted disease."

"Serves her right," she mouths, smirking at me.

"I feel for the kid though. Because he ditched her, of course, and she ended up dropping out of school. I know what kind of life that can be for a kid."

"No parents?" she asks, her delicious lips my main focus.

"They kicked her out because she had 'sullied their good name' or some bullshit like that."

"Seems like a harsh punishment for a childish prank," she quietly says. At my look, she touches her throat and shakes her head.

"Just because it's feeling better doesn't mean you should talk, sweetheart."

She shrugs, grinning.

"So I said all of that to say this, you're not her in any way, stretch, or form. Would...do you want to see where this goes?"

At her nod, I lean in and kiss her thoroughly. While I want her with every fiber of my being, I've waited this long for someone like her, so I can wait a little while longer. Today was so emotional, I want her to be fully engaged, not worrying about Honor.

Pulling back, I ask, "Okay, so I pulled up *The Lord of the Rings*. You interested?"

At her nod, I get us settled so she's curled into me, finally at peace with my shitty past.

CHAPTER NINETEEN

Delaney

I slowly wake up to find myself nestled with my face in the crook of Asa's neck. In sleep, he looks younger, as though the shit he's gone through never happened. As I replay everything that happened the day before, especially how he cared for me last night, I realize how much I want to be his. Easing away from him, I get out of bed and quietly go into the bathroom. Once I've taken care of business and washed up, I head back to the bed and slide in next to him.

"You okay?" he mumbles, his eyes still closed.

"Yeah," I whisper, amazed at how much better my throat already feels.

One eye pops open to glare at me because I spoke. "Delaney," he warns.

"Kiss me, Asa, make me yours," I boldly say.

Inside, my heart is beating so quickly I'm pretty sure I'm heading for a heart attack, but if yesterday showed me anything, it's that life is too damn short, nothing is guaranteed. I want him, with every fiber of my being.

"Those are two different things, Pixie," he replies. "One isn't inclusive of the other. If I make you mine, you're stuck with me. No take backs."

"No take backs," I agree. "So, hopefully, I don't suck at it, because you'd be stuck with me."

He chuckles before kissing me deeply. I lose track of time as we thoroughly learn one another's mouths, until he finally pulls back, both of us panting slightly. "Since I've never had this in a relationship before, we're learning together, sweetheart," he says.

"No relationships since high school?" I murmur.

"One-night stands aren't considered relationships. Just know it's been a long time since one of those has happened."

I nod because after all, he's a single guy, good looking on top of that, and he rides a Harley. All of those things are magnets for women, and for me to think he's been celibate his whole life is ridiculous. Men don't attach the same importance as some women do to keeping themselves for that special person. Regardless, I'll never hold his past against him; it's not who I am at all.

"Gotcha. Well, you'll be boldly going where no man has gone before," I tease, trying to settle my nerves.

While Honor shared about her night with me, it's a different thing altogether when you're the one in the hot seat, so to speak. Just as I begin to say something to fill the silence, since I don't know what to do next, he kisses me again.

"If all we do is this until you're ready, that's okay too," he whispers against my lips. "Won't make you any less mine, Delaney."

"I want more," I insist. "Just… if I start to ramble, kiss me and get me out of my head. I'll overthink all of it otherwise."

"Why?" he asks, genuinely curious.

"Because I grew up never being good enough, Asa. It took Honor coming into my life for me to realize that I was fine just the way I was. I mean, my aunt and uncle are great and love me, faults and all, but my parents? Not so much. I didn't do a lot right in their eyes. It's why we're estranged," I admit.

"Well, you've got me now, and my brothers, as well as

Honor's extended family in South Carolina. You'll never be alone again."

Feeling his body heat so close to me has me throwing caution to the wind. Reaching up, I pull his face closer to mine and initiate a kiss, all while moving so I'm practically sprawled on top of him, his erection resting hot and hard against my low abdomen. As his hands stroke up my sides, they take his T-shirt with them until I'm bared to his gaze. Instead of shrinking in on myself in an effort to hide my erect nipples and swollen breasts, I revel in the look in his eyes as he looks his fill before reverently reaching up and cupping them.

"Fucking perfection," he murmurs, leaning up slightly to take one nipple between his lips. As heat courses through my body to pool at the apex of my thighs, I unconsciously grind against him, whimpering when it doesn't yield any tangible results. He alternates from side to side until both nipples are swollen with need and I'm whiny with need.

Before I realize what's happening, he's flipped us so I'm on my back and he's hovering over me. Instinctively, I know that what we're doing now is unlike any other time he's had sex before; it's in the set of his jaw and how he's holding himself so taut, as though he's trying not to lose control.

But I hope he does at some point. Hell, who am I kidding? I'll take whatever he wants to give me and probably beg for more at this point. I can feel my clit pulsing and he's stayed above the waist so far!

"Ready for more?" he questions, his gaze holding mine. At my nod, he slides the shorts he lent me down my hips until they're puddled at the end of the bed, and I'm sprawled there, as naked as the day I was born. He's got a slight smile on his face as his eyes dip to the apex of my thighs and I know he's seeing the evidence of my arousal. "If I do anything you don't like, you say the word, do you understand?" he asks, moving down until he's settled between my thighs. "Anything at all, Delaney, I mean it."

"I understand," I whisper. When I feel his breath waft across my heated core, I barely hold back the shudder that wants to break free. Just that slight touch, which wasn't even a touch at that, has me wanting to splay my legs completely open and let him have his way with me.

Without warning, he leans in and swipes his tongue through my folds, moaning slightly as he tastes me for the first time. My self-consciousness now gone, I allow myself to feel what he's doing to me. He sets a steady pace, ending each time with a slight suckle of my clit, which I'm positive is distended and pulsing at this point. When he slips his index finger inside, we both groan although I'm sure it's for entirely different reasons.

"So fucking tight," he murmurs, glancing up at me. As my gaze captures his, he grins, then flicks his tongue against my clit while his finger slowly thrusts in and out of my sheath.

I may be a virgin, but I've gotten myself off with my vibrator, and nothing could've prepared me for the difference in orgasms. As mine rushes up to overtake me, he inserts a second finger, while I keen out his name, my back bowing off the bed.

"Holy shit," I say when I'm able to clearly think once again. His chuckle against my pussy has me clenching against his fingers, which he slowly withdraws then proceeds to lick clean. "That's the hottest thing I think I've ever seen," I admit.

He reaches over to his nightstand and pulls out a condom, which is good because I'm not currently on birth control. Within seconds, he has his cock encased in the rubber and he's notching himself at my entrance. Slowly, watching me the whole time, he enters me, inch by inch. The slight stretch and burn isn't anything I didn't expect, but I briefly worry about the pain I'm about to feel.

Leaning in, he captures my lips with his and as I bury my hands in his hair to pull him closer, he finally bottoms out, leaving me feeling so full, I think I might combust. "You good?" he asks against my lips. At my nod, he slowly pulls out then thrusts back inside until he has a steady pace going.

"Wrap your legs around my waist," he encourages, panting. When I do as he asks, he goes impossibly deeper, hitting another spot inside that has me seeing stars as my pussy clenches around his cock. "Fuck, you do that again and I won't be able to keep from coming."

"It feels good, Asa, so so good," I whisper.

As I start moving with him, feeling the build of another orgasm, he increases the tempo, sweat now dripping down his forehead and hitting me on the chest. I detonate when his thumb reaches between us and applies pressure against my clit, screaming out his name, uncaring that my throat is once again hurting.

He thrusts several more times then stops, calling out my name, and I can feel his cock pulsing inside me as my pussy clenches his length. Long moments pass as he remains suspended above me before he rolls us so I'm laying on top of him, somehow still connected.

"We're doing that again soon, right?" I rasp out, causing him to glare at me.

Only... he can't manage it for too long before he starts laughing. "I want to yell at you for screaming because I know you hurt yourself again, but I'm so fucking relaxed right now, I can't make myself do it," he finally sputters out.

"Sorry," I murmur. "Didn't mean to."

"I know, babe. And to answer your question, we'll do that as often as you want," he says, grinning up at me as he pushes my wayward curls away from my face. "Looks like another shower's in order before we grab a bite to eat. I'm sure you want to go see Honor."

Guilt briefly swamps me; while we were making love, she never once crossed my mind. What kind of friend does that make me?

"She may not want to talk," he warns as we walk hand in hand toward her room.

"That's fine. I have a few things I want to say," I quietly reply.

"Well, go easy on her, Delaney. Neither of us experienced what she did, remember? So, we don't know where her head's at."

"It's not with us, the people who love her," I hiss. Yeah, I'm angry at her. But I'm also feeling guilty about the whole thing as well, so there's that. Hell, maybe I need fucking counseling.

When we reach her room, I see Patsy and her service dog sitting on one side of the bed, and Patsy's quietly talking. Asa kisses me and motions for me to head inside.

"What about you?" I whisper.

"She needs you girls first, sweetheart. I'll run and grab some drinks, okay?" he replies.

"Yeah, that works."

I walk over to the bed and sit down on the opposite side of where Patsy's at, taking Honor's hand in mine and leaning down to kiss her forehead. She's still unconscious, or sedated, whatever terminology they want to use. "Hey, wench, seems to me, you got some 'splaining to do," I whisper.

Patsy nods then starts talking, looking at Honor the whole time. "When I was a teenager, I was diagnosed with depression and body dysmorphia. The day I listened to the voices, my best friend, CeeCee, found me and saved my life, just like Delaney did with you. Honor, I know you haven't been seeing Dr. Williams, we called her office and they have never seen you. Now, before you bitch about patient confidentiality, we asked in such a way that it seemed like you forgot when your appointment was, and the receptionist said something along the lines of they were glad you were finally coming in. Here's the thing, when I was assaulted by a coworker, I started spiraling again. It was Dr. Williams who got me turned around, babe. She's the one who gave me some suggestions about what to do so I could fight back. Then Atlas got me Ridley." She reaches down and pats her dog, who perked up at its name.

"I said all that to say this, I've been where you are right now, Honor. I know that you think there's no way anyone would ever want to be involved with you ever again. That you're dirty, a slut, a whore. *None* of those things are truth, Honor. Not one word of it. The right man, whether it's Savage or someone else, isn't going to give a fuck that you were assaulted in that way. Except, of course, to understand you will probably have triggers and learn how to navigate around them. A healthy, happy sex life is possible again. You may not see it right now and that's okay. It's more important that we get your head straight first. I'm not a doctor, but I'm willing to bet that what happened to you, coupled with your medical condition, has caused you to slip into depression. Dr. Williams can help with that, sweetheart, and I hope like hell you'll let her. Because the world would be a darker place without you here."

By the time Patsy's done talking, I'm crying again, the tears slipping down my face to sprinkle Honor's hand. When I feel her flinch, I look up at her to see her eyes open and staring at me, her own eyes wet with unshed tears.

"I'm sorry," she rasps out, her voice husky from everything they did to her to save her life.

CHAPTER TWENTY

Glacier

When I walk back into Honor's room, I see she's awake, which loosens the stranglehold that was on my heart. Handing Delaney a drink, I lean down and kiss her head before moving closer to Honor and hugging her.

"We need to call Gunner, tell him what happened," I tell her.

"No! Please, Asa, we can't call him. He'll freak out."

"Ya think?" I retort. "Jesus, Honor, you have no fucking clue how close you came to dying, do you?"

She looks embarrassed, but I push through. "Your fucking heart stopped, did you know that? And you had to have *two* blood transfusions, for fuck's sake."

"Asa," Delaney says, trying to stop me.

Turning to her, I shake my head. "No, she needs to hear this, babe." Looking back at Honor, I steel my heart against the tears steadily trickling down her face. "It's been me and you against the world since we were kids, squirt. How do you think I feel knowing I *failed*?"

"You didn't fail me, Asa," she murmurs, her eyes now downcast.

"Yeah, I fucking did. You weren't seeing the therapist like you told us you were. I brought you here because this is what you said you needed, Honor. How in the hell am I supposed to face your brother knowing I nearly had to call him to tell him you were dead?"

"I'm sorry," she whispers.

"Asa, what if we go in with her to therapy? At least until she's comfortable with Dr. Williams?" Delaney suggest.

"The only way I'll agree to not call Gunner is if you do this, Honor," I tell her. "Something's gotta give and I get you're still feeling some kind of way inside, but if you don't let someone help you, the next time you might not be as fortunate."

"Okay, yes, I'll see her, and you can go with me, either one of you, it doesn't matter. I... I don't know if I want you in the room with me, but I might at some point," she says. "I... I know I scared y'all yesterday, and if I could do it over again, I'd rethink my choice."

"You probably wouldn't," Patsy interjects, causing me to glare at her. "What? She probably wouldn't, Glacier, and if you're honest with yourself, you'll agree at some point. Honor, you've hit rock bottom. Now there's no other way but up and while you're going to think we're nothing but pains in your ass, you bought that ticket, you understand? Coddling is now over, tough love is in session."

Delaney giggles as Patsy is trying so hard to be stern, but I can see the concern on her face. "You and me baby, we're stuck like glue," she sing-songs, squeezing Honor's fingers.

"Fine, fine. Let's find out when I'm getting out of here so I can see Dr. Williams."

"About that, you're on a seventy-two-hour psych hold, Honor, because of the circumstances behind your admittance," I tell her. "I think you'll see the hospital's psychiatrist, or maybe it's psychologist, but until they sign off, you're stuck in here."

"I brought you some things," Delaney says. "Your pajamas, your phone and charger, personal hygiene items, that sort of stuff. If there's anything I forgot, just let me know."

She looks at my woman and smiles. "Thank you. I don't deserve you, or Asa, hell, any of y'all at this point. I've been a selfish, whiny bitch about it all."

"Hold up now, you endured a traumatic assault. Your feelings are neither right nor wrong," Patsy states. "The only thing you did incorrectly was not accept the help that's been available. There's nothing wrong with being a bit selfish as you heal, and you sure as hell never whine about a damn thing."

"Alright, so we're agreed? We don't tell Gunner," Honor asks. "I'll do whatever they tell me to do and yeah, I'll put in the work so I can get better. I… I got scared after I did it, but by then, I was fading so I couldn't call for help. I'm glad you found me, Delaney, but I'm so fucking sorry it was like that."

Delaney shrugs as though it wasn't a big deal, but I can hear the echo of her screams in my head, and visualize how shattered she was last night in the shower, so I'm not quite as forgiving.

"You should be, Honor," I tell her, gentling my voice slightly at the look on her face. "Trust me, your bathroom looks like a slasher film."

I see her glance at her bandaged wrists, a grimace on her face as she nods.

"We need to go clean that up!" Delaney exclaims.

"No, you don't. Granny and Mama M had the prospects do it yesterday while y'all were at the hospital," Patsy says. "Honor, if you'll tell me your size, I'll look for some lightweight long-sleeve shirts for you."

"So, you're claiming an ol' lady, huh?" Atlas asks as we walk into church.

"Looks that way," I reply, smirking.

He slaps me on the shoulder and says, "Good for you. Think she's gonna fit in here just fine."

His words bring me up short. Delaney and I haven't even discussed the future, but I want her here. With me. Looks like we need to have a talk later on today.

As we sit around the table waiting on Poseidon to bring us to order, my mind drifts over what happened after we got back from the hospital. Since Honor is under the psych hold, she's undergoing extensive testing and even some counseling, so we weren't able to stay. We left with a list of things she wanted as well as a promise that we'd get them up to her.

"Alright, y'all, let's get this done and dusted, so we can get back to work," Poseidon commands, hitting the gavel on the table. All conversation ceases, and we focus on him. "Orion, can you go over the finances?" he asks.

Orion covers all our businesses, as well as what that'll mean to our wallets.

I'm just a patched member, not an officer, so I don't get as big of a cut, but because of the increase in custom helmets due to my designs, I am seeing a bump which is nice. Right now, my expenses are minimal at best; clothes, my cell phone, stuff for my bike. Which means I've managed to bank a significant amount of money and it may be time for me to talk to Poseidon about one of the other houses on the property. While all of us have our own suite of rooms in the main building, the brothers who've started a family have their own homes. Some were completely built, others were renovations that were done on the existing structures. I'm torn about what I'd like; guess it depends on what Delaney tells me later.

"Specks, I take it you're helping the DRMC track down the fuckers who hurt Honor," Poseidon states, pulling me back into the conversation and away from my own thoughts.

"I've offered my assistance, but get the impression they've got it under control," Specks replies. "Still, I have several searches running and will forward anything I find to them since it's likely those assholes are still up there."

"Well, I've let Hammer know if he needs us when they find them to let us know, we'll be happy to help since she's family to us as well," Poseidon says. "Atlas, heard anything out of Nick yet?"

I turn to my friend, knowing he had planned to reach out to the Black Tuxedos dog trainer for Honor. I hope he does find one that'll work for her; I know it'll give her the independence she's fought so hard for while also allowing Gunner and Savage to ease off the stranglehold I'm positive they'll put on her once she's ready to go back home.

"He's got feelers out. You know how he likes to work, get a couple of dogs that might do the job then get the person there so he can see which one will be the best match," Atlas replies. "Speaking of, how was she today?" he asks, looking at me.

"Well, I may or may not have torn her a new one about her decision yesterday," I admit, rubbing my hand across my face. "Then, once I got it all out, she said she realized too late she'd made a mistake only she was close to passing out and couldn't call for help."

"Fucking miracle that Delaney went in at just the right time to ask her something," Trident murmurs, with the other brothers nodding in agreement.

"Yeah, that's one call I would've hated making," I say. "I wanted to call him today, but she promises she'll see the counselor, and with the psych hold they've got her on, I'm sure they'll have a list of checks and balances to keep her honest."

Poseidon sighs. "Fuck, Brother, not sure what to say right now. I mean, personally, I think he deserves to know. If it were me and I had a sister who nearly died by her own hand, I'd be pissed as hell if I wasn't told. But she knows her brother best, I guess."

"He'd put her under lock and key, Pres," I admit. "He's pretty fucking intense, and having to wait all those years for her to be with him again because of the stupid fucking system, I can't say as I blame him. I expect a fist to the face at the very least."

"He can go through us first," Brooks decrees.

"Well, let's see how it plays out. Now, is there something else I need to know?" he asks, smirking at me.

"Asked Delaney to be mine last night and she said yes," I say. "Not sure how that'll work, though, because I know she's got a job in South Carolina."

"Brother, she took a leave of absence and is now

working as a substitute for our school system," Specks advises. "Sounds like she'd be amenable to staying here."

"Get with me, presume you're not going to want to stay at the clubhouse if she does decide to stay," Poseidon orders.

"Will do, Pres."

"Anything else?" he questions, looking around the table. "Okay, good. Keep up the good work, we have two new prospects, Billy and Frank, but could use a few more."

With that, he bangs his gavel once again, dismissing us.

As we head into the common room, I see Delaney sitting with the ol' ladies and head in her direction. Once I reach her, I lean down, kiss her then ask, "You wanna go for a ride?"

Her eyes light up and she replies, "On your bike?"

"Yeah."

She nods so I help her up. "Let's go get you ready for the ride, Pixie."

CHAPTER TWENTY-ONE

Delaney

Honor's been back at the clubhouse for two weeks now and already, I can see a marked difference. She was started on antidepressants while still in the hospital, plus she sees Dr. Williams twice a week. While the sessions definitely wear her out, and despite the nightmares that continue every night like clockwork, she acts as though she's sorting things out. Today, while the guys are out on a ride, we're hanging at the inside pool, laughing at the kids' antics.

"He's hysterical," I tell Kaya, as Noah 'fights off' imaginary sea monsters so the younger kids can freely swim.

"You have no idea," she retorts. "I swear to God, Specks is going to have to replace the subfloor in the house if he and Noah keep up with their epic sea battles in the tub."

"He's a good kid," Hayley defends, smiling over at her son. "They're all good kids."

"Yeah, they are," Gia agrees.

"Honor, what are you guys going to do later?" Patsy asks. At Honor's look of surprise, she continues. "What I mean is, other than therapy, you've been stuck to the clubhouse like glue. Maybe the two of you should go shopping. We're having some great sales at the store!"

"I'm game if you are," I tell her. I feel a little guilty because since that first night, I've spent every night in Asa's bed, our limbs entwined. I'm close but not adjoining room close any longer. However, she hasn't said anything about it, so I won't either.

"Let's make it a girl's trip!" CeeCee exclaims. "I'm sure there are things we could all use, if not for ourselves, then for our men or the kids."

"And who are we gonna corral to watch the kids?" Lilli asks.

"Well, let's see, we've got your mother-in-law, Patsy's mom, Kaya's grandmother, Mary and Shamus, Tessie, plus two prospects. Seems like that's enough to wrangle thirteen kids," Gia sasses. "And it's not like we'd be gone forever. It'd be the perfect ending to a Saturday."

"Oh, maybe we can talk the guys into cooking out tomorrow? Kind of a last gasp sort of thing?" Patsy asks.

"We'll make it happen," Lilli decrees, pulling out her phone and sending a text. "There, my man will make it so," she says, laughing.

"Did you have fun today?" Asa asks as we get out of the shower. I'm blushing but I'm not sure if it's because I gave him a blowjob or the steam.

"Yeah, it was good to see Honor laughing."

"Heard from Savage again. Not sure how much longer I can hold him and Gunner off," he replies, taking a towel and thoroughly drying me off.

Now that my skin is tingling, the last thing I want to discuss is that hornet's nest, but considering it's our life right now, I continue to listen as I begin brushing out my hair.

Asa takes the brush away and guides me toward the bed. "You know I enjoy brushing your hair," he reminds me, settling me between his muscular thighs. I can feel him hardening against my back and bite back a grin, knowing how this is going to play out.

"How long do you think we've got? I know she's made some progress, but she's not ready to go home yet," I tell him, closing my eyes and biting back a moan. I love having my hair played with and the fact that he likes taking care of such a menial task for me makes me love him even more.

Wait… love? No. It's too soon, way too soon. Hell, we haven't discussed what happens when she *is* ready to go home yet!

"What has you so quiet, babe?" he asks, leaning in and whispering in my ear.

"We haven't talked about what happens when she's ready to go home," I quietly state. "Plus, I uh, well, how I feel about you smacked me square in the face," I admit.

He turns me so I'm straddling his lap and cups my face in his hands. Knowing how he is about touch, I love that he's unbothered with me. In fact, when we're together, we're always touching in some capacity.

"I was kind of hoping you'd want to stay here," he says. "I know you're on leave from your job in South Carolina, but you found a substitute teaching position here. Maybe they'll offer you a job, or you can keep substituting and find kids to tutor. Doesn't matter to me, whatever makes you happy."

"You wouldn't care if I didn't work full time?" I ask.

"Babe, I've been with the club for several years now and have little in the way of expenses. I live at the clubhouse, I'm now a patched member so my paycheck has increased, plus with every custom helmet order that's sold, I get a bonus. I've got plenty to cover us," he says. "I just want you here with me."

"I want to stay here with you, Asa. I'm falling in love with you," I reply.

"Good to know, Pixie, because you managed to do the impossible. You thawed out my cold, dead heart and made me realize I wanted what my brothers all have. In case that wasn't clear, I've fallen in love with you. If you decided you wanted to go back to South Carolina, I'd ask Poseidon if he would talk to Hammer so I could switch clubs. Wouldn't be my first choice, but that's how strongly I feel about us."

By now, my eyes are watering because with everyone else, he's somewhat of an introvert. He speaks, but not unless he's asked a question, and then he never expounds on it all that much. He just answers whoever asked then shuts up. But with me, conversation is never an issue. We don't have to fill the quiet times, but we have no issues finding things to talk about either and

I'm finding out so much more than I ever knew when it comes to this unique, challenging disorder. I'm grateful he took a leap of faith with me, and I quietly vow that he'll never regret making that choice.

"If I don't stop this, you're going to think all I do is cry," I mumble, wiping away the stray tears that have fallen.

"I know better, Delaney. Now, give me a kiss so I can finish brushing your hair," he demands.

Laughing, I lean in and give him a peck on the lips before I quickly spin around and sit between his legs once again.

"Little minx," he grumbles, but there's laughter in his tone and my heart smiles knowing I'm the one who put it there.

———⇇———

"It gets better every single time," I gasp out, flopping down onto my stomach with Asa pressing me into the mattress. "I think that's my new favorite position."

He chuckles, kissing my sweaty shoulder. "You said that when you rode me, too."

"Oh, yeah, that one's up there, but this one has you hitting my G-spot. I swear to God I saw the space station when I came."

His chuckles turn into full-blown laughter as he maneuvers us so we're face-to-face. "God, I love you. You have no idea just how much."

"Probably as much as I do you," I reply, kissing the underside of his jaw.

"Let me get you cleaned up so we can get some sleep."

"Okay."

That's another thing he does that has endeared him to me. Once we had the talk, we both got tested and I got the implant so we could forego condoms. The sensation is unlike anything I ever expected, but it's definitely messier. However, he always makes sure a towel's down before anything gets too out of control, then he cleans me up before we go to sleep. It may not last forever, but the care he takes with me is something I've come to cherish.

CHAPTER TWENTY-TWO

Glacier

"Savage, you're gonna have to chill out," I say through the phone.

It's been three months since Honor came back with me and every single week, I tell him the same fucking thing. I'm pretty sure by now he's close to losing his shit, but there's so much he's not aware of, stuff I haven't shared because of the promise I made to Honor. Since she's kept her word and is diligently working in therapy, I've stuck to mine as well.

"I'm done waiting around," he retorts. "And you're not talking me out of it this time either. Don't know if you've got voodoo magic or some bullshit, but it's not happening."

"You need to give her a bit more time. I keep telling you."

"And I keep telling you, Glacier. This time I'm done fuckin' around. It's been three months. Three fuckin' months of you giving us updates. I want to see her for myself. Bring her home where she belongs. *I need to be the one to help her.* I didn't fight when she needed to get out of here. I know it's on us. On the club what she went through, but none of us can fix shit when she's not around for us to do that," he growls out, frustration evident in every word.

"Savage, there's shit you all don't know. Shit she's trying to work through."

"I don't give a damn."

"You should," I grunt out. It's the closest I've come to giving up Honor's secrets, but truthfully, I'm tired of being Savage's punching bag. Granted, it's verbal versus physical, but still, I've taken a lot of shit on her behalf which wouldn't be happening if she would've let me clue Gunner in to the situation.

"Why, because she's better off without any of us?" he questions.

"Didn't say that," I mumble. "I know where she belongs, where she should be, but mentally, she's in a completely different zone altogether. She's not ready to face what happened to her." I pause then sigh before continuing. "You want to know the truth, man, she's been in a dark as fuck place, so damn dark, if not for the ol' ladies to my brothers helping her alongside Delaney, she wouldn't be here and I'm *not* talking figuratively."

And that's as close as I'll get to letting the cat out of the bag, but from the silence on the other end of the phone, I'm pretty sure he understands what I didn't say.

"I'm coming to get her," Savage bites out before disconnecting the phone.

Guess I better give Gunner a head's up that his man's heading in our direction. Poseidon too, while I'm thinking about it. First things first, though. Scrolling through my phone, I hit Gunner's number then wait until he picks up.

"Man, can you hold Savage off a little longer?" I ask once he answers. "He just told me he was done waiting and he's on his way, Gun. She still needs time."

"Right. It's his decision and I agree with him. Been long enough away from my sister. Know she's with you, Glacier, but I've got to make things right with Honor and I can't do that when she's fuckin' hours away from me," Gunner replies.

"I'll let Pres know, but Gunner, if she's not ready to go when y'all get here, y'all better not force the issue. The ol' ladies have grown fond of her, and I'd hate for y'all to have to go up against them," I retort.

He chuckles, but there's no real humor behind his laugh when he says, "We'll be there soon."

Fuck my life. Sighing, I head out of my workroom and move toward Atlas' office so I can let him know the current state of affairs. This is either going to go one of two ways; it'll be a total shitshow, or they'll realize I've been telling them the truth.

As I step into the room, Atlas glances up at me and says, "Poseidon just texted. Seems we're going to have some visitors in a few hours. Better go tell your ol' lady at least, Brother."

"Yeah, looking forward to that conversation," I reply. He barks out a laugh and motions for me to go.

"Gunner, Savage," I call out the moment the two men step across the threshold.

Savage jerks his chin at me before he asks, "Where's Honor?"

"She's in her room," I reply, going on alert.

"You tell her we were coming?" Gunner asks.

"No." I shake my head and continue. "Delaney and I took her out for a little while today. We just got back a bit ago and she said she was tired and was going to go lay down."

"Right." Savage nods, but I can tell he seems unsettled which puts me on edge.

"Savage, she needs time to rest," Delaney murmurs, stepping up next to Glacier, looking nervous.

"Someone want to fill us in on what's going on?" Gunner growls, placing a hand on Savage's shoulder.

"There's nothing to fill you in on," Delaney mutters.

"Then where's my fuckin' woman's room?" he demands through gritted teeth.

"Honor's not your woman." Delaney narrows her eyes and glares at him, causing me to smirk.

"Bullshit, Delaney, and you know it. I made it known at the hospital she was mine before she even woke up. Don't try to keep me from her now. I haven't seen her in three fuckin' months and I'm not about to be kept from her any longer. Now where the fuck is she?"

I can feel the anger coursing off him and glance around the room to see my brothers have spread out, keeping the women back until the situation fully reveals itself.

"Savage, "I start before I'm interrupted.

"There's things that you don't know," Patsy says, stepping forward. Her eyes are filled with empathy as she looks from me to Delaney. "He should know what he's dealing with."

I nod before wrapping an arm around Delaney and pulling her into my side while glancing between Gunner and Savage. "A month ago, Honor slit her wrists, trying to kill herself. Before that, she attempted to overdose."

"The fuck did you just say?" Savage demands, his fists clenching and unclenching at his sides. Right now, he looks like he wants to hit something and if the shoe was on the other foot, I can't say I wouldn't feel the same fucking way.

"You wanna tell me why I wasn't told about this?" Gunner sneers at the same time.

"She didn't want you to know," Delaney whispers.

"You have to understand," the dark-haired woman starts.

"I don't have to understand shit. Where the fuck is my woman?" Savage steps forwards and Atlas steps up and wraps an arm around Patsy's waist and pulls her back into him, glaring at Savage to back the fuck off. Savage doesn't, glaring at the pair in return, trying to get them to look away or crumble and give him what he wants.

But she doesn't look away nor does she back down. "Savage, you need to calm down. You say she's your woman, if that's true then you need to take a moment and listen to me. She didn't want you to know because she's embarrassed by what she tried to do to herself. That she nearly took her own life. I know how she feels. I've been there. Honor is in a seriously dark place and I'm willing to bet that the only way to really pull her out is if you help her, but you have to be calm about it. You can't storm in there and be all he-man on her."

"I'm not going to do that shit," Savage spits out. He takes in a deep, shuddering breath before looking at me and asks, "Where's her room?"

I stare at him for a moment before answering. "Hallway off to the right, go down mid-way and her door is on the left. It'll be unlocked as she made a deal she wouldn't lock herself in the room."

Several of us keep Gunner company while Savage is with Honor. He keeps glaring at me until I finally say, "You have one shot, man."

"What?" he asks.

"You get one punch, then I'll fight back."

"Why the fuck would I punch you?" he questions.

"Just figured you'd want to since I kept that information from you is all," I reply, shrugging.

He huffs out a laugh. "Part of me wants to, but I get it. You've been there for her when I wasn't able to be, all the way back to when y'all were kids. I know how stubborn my sister can be, Glace, so she probably swore you to secrecy or some shit."

I smirk while nodding. "Pretty much. But actually, she freaked out so bad the day after when she woke up and I tore her a new one then told her I was calling you, I was afraid it might set her back, y'know?"

"You tore her a new one?" he asks, admiration in his tone.

"Oh yeah he did," Delaney adds, grinning at me. "I thought he was a bit too hard, but he got her to understand that if she had been successful, and let me be clear here, it very nearly was, she would've devastated a lot of people."

"Well, damn, cuz, I'm impressed," Gunner says. A noise at the entrance to the hall has him looking up, a grin splitting his face as Honor rushes toward him.

"C'mon, Pixie, let's give them some time together," I say as the two of them start whispering to each other.

"Okay."

Taking my woman's hand in mine, I walk over to where Atlas and Patsy are sitting, their daughter ensconced in his muscular arms, sound asleep and drooling on his cut. "Appreciate what you did earlier, Patsy," I tell her.

"I was never in agreement with not telling them what she attempted, but it wasn't my call to make," she says. "However, it's obvious both of those men love her, and they've been suffering for three months not knowing what's going on. Now, everyone knows so there'll be no more secrets and she can hopefully continue moving forward in her healing."

"I'm grateful that you know how she feels," Delaney adds. "Not that you've gone through that shit, of course, but I couldn't reach her, and neither could Asa. You having the experience and obviously being successful in your own healing journey did more than anything I could've ever told her myself."

"She just lost her way for a little while is all," Patsy says. "Besides, from what I've been observing, I think those two men will move heaven and earth to slay her demons and help her continue to heal. Don't be surprised if Dr. Williams tells her she thinks it's time for her to go home."

The shattered look on Delaney's face has me pulling her into my arms. "You knew it was going to happen, babe," I whisper.

"I know, but being faced with it as a reality instead of a future event is hitting me more than I anticipated," she admits.

"Come on, let's go for a ride," I say. "Wind therapy always makes things make sense."

CHAPTER TWENTY-THREE

Delaney

True to his word, Asa took me for a ride. We ended up a little further down the coast, then walked down to the beach so we could watch the waves ebb and flow. There's something calming about seeing the constant predictability of something so vast that's controlled by the pull of the moon.

"Have you decided which house you want or whether you just want to build one?" he asks.

"I really like the one that looks like a cottage," I reply, thinking about the sprawling house that's tucked into the woods.

It's got four bedrooms and two baths, and the exterior is stone, something I really love. The inside is homey and cozy, and I can picture Asa and I puttering around inside after spending an evening at the clubhouse. Heat rises in my face as I remember the fantasies I had surrounding the fireplace.

"I like it as well. There's plenty of room for us to raise a family, plus there's a dedicated room you can use as an office," he says.

"A family? You want kids?"

"I want kids with *you*," he states, kissing my temple. "Before, well, I never saw myself with an ol' lady much less wanting to have a family of my own. But with you, I want it all, babe. The good, the bad, the ugly."

"Hopefully, there'll be more good than bad or ugly," I tease, turning so I'm fully facing him. "So, you really think she'll be going back soon?"

"Yeah, I do. I don't see her brother or Savage wanting to stay around indefinitely. I'm pretty sure Dr. Williams will give her a list of doctors for her to continue her therapy, but she needs to get back to home and allow their club to help her heal."

"I haven't told her I want to stay," I murmur. "I mean, I'd need to go back long enough to get all the rest of my stuff, and resign from my job, but other than that, my home is here with you now."

Turning me, he cups my face in the way I've grown to

love and kisses me thoroughly. Once we're both breathless, he pulls back slightly and says, "We'll make that trip happen whenever you want, Pixie."

"I need to make a list of things I have to take care of," I reply, grinning up at him. For the first time since everything happened that led us to St. Marys, I feel settled inside.

"Whatever you need to do is what we'll do," he states. "Want to stop for some ice cream on our way back home?"

"You don't like ice cream," I remind him, giggling.

"No, but I like watching you eat it," he teases, waggling his brows at me. "Gives me a lot of good ideas."

I laugh so hard I snort before finally choking out, "Sounds like a guy thing for sure."

"Absolutely."

Honor took Savage with her today to the therapist and I've been waiting on pins and needles ever since to find out how it went. I'm still a bit reserved where he's concerned, but I need to remember my best friend has a good head on her shoulders.

When they finally get back, I rush over to her. "How did it go?" I ask.

"It went okay," she says, looking nervous. Taking a deep breath, she continues. "Dr. Williams thinks I should go home."

"Oh." I blink at her, my eyes widening as tears threaten before I glance over at Asa. Looking back at Honor, I ask, "Are you going to?"

Her gaze on Savage, she then turns to me and replies, "As much as the idea scares me and I'm not sure I'm exactly ready, she's right."

I shrug because I know she's right deep down inside, but still, ever since we met, we've been together. This will be something different for both of us, that's for damn sure.

"Let's go to my room," she suggests, guessing this is something we need to talk about in private.

I nod and the two of us head to her room. Inside we both curl up on the bed, sitting crossed legged in front of each other.

"You don't want to go back home do you?" she blurts out and again, I nod.

"I really like it here," I whisper. "I really like him."

Okay, I love him, but first things first, this is her cousin after all and she's been so focused on herself, she hasn't exactly been paying attention to the two of us.

"I know you do. I can see it in your face." She smiles at me before saying, "If you want to stay, stay. Talk to Glacier and tell him. But Dr. Williams is right that to overcome what happened I need to face it."

"But isn't it too fast?" I ask, my concern for her overriding my need to be with him.

"Maybe." She shrugs. "I know I'm not ready to face it. I don't think I ever will be, but I'm hiding out here and she says I need to find a normal for me. I won't be able to do that unless I'm back home."

"Are you going to do that with Savage?" I question.

"Honestly I don't know. He confuses me, but he opened up to me about some things and I trust him. He makes me feel safe."

"Last night you didn't scream in your sleep," I murmur, surprising her.

We spend some more time talking before heading back out to everyone else. Unsurprisingly, we end up at the pool, with Gunner and Savage getting in on the insanity the kids employ when it comes to sea creatures and keeping everyone safe.

Later that night, curled in Asa's arms, I murmur, "I'm going to miss her, you know."

"It's not as if you'll never see each other again, Delaney," he replies, his hand running through my hair. "You're going to have to go back and get shit sorted out with your old job, that kind of thing. If you want to go by yourself, that's fine, or we can go up together. Totally up to you."

"I think I want you with me."

"Then that's what we'll do."

It takes a few more days, but finally, the three of them are heading out, Honor behind Savage as they roar out of the parking lot. Taking my hand, Asa pulls me over to one of the side-by-sides that they use on the property. "Let's go check our house out, babe. See what we're going to need, okay?"

I swear that despite the short time we've been together, he just gets me, knowing I need to do something else to keep busy, so I don't break down in tears. I know Honor and I'll talk frequently, but it's not the same as popping into each other's rooms.

As we bounce along the path toward where our house is situated, I take stock of how much my life has changed in such a short amount of time. I went from being single, happy in the career I built, and content to let life move along, to the ol' lady of a biker who had every reason to keep himself closed off from the world based on how he'd been treated.

"How did I get so lucky?" I ask as we finally pull in front of the house.

"The better question is, how did I?" he replies, taking my hand as we walk up the path. "Everything I went through, all the shit that was shoveled at me, it was all worth it since you were at the end of the journey."

"I think… I think that's the sweetest thing anyone's ever said to me," I say. "Thank you for being willing to take a chance on us, Asa. Because I can honestly say I couldn't imagine being with anyone else besides you."

"Thank your cousin, Pixie. She's the one who wanted the two of us to meet," he teases. "Granted, I think I'd have preferred better circumstances, but still, the end result is the same. You're mine and I'm yours."

CHAPTER TWENTY-FOUR

Glacier

"Delaney, are you sure we need all this?" I ask as we head to the checkout at Buc-ee's. Ever since Honor called to tell us she was pregnant, Delaney's been buying stuff for the baby. I actually thought she was done, but I was obviously mistaken based on the cart full of baby items with the store's mascot on them.

"Yes, I'm sure," she replies. "Plus, I got her some of her favorite saltwater taffy. I know she has to be careful with how much she eats because of the diabetes, but she said her doctor and she were happy with where her numbers have been lately."

Instead of rolling my eyes, which I apparently picked up from all the women at the club, I help her unload the stuff onto the counter, grateful I decided to bring my truck. Gunner's ol' lady and several of the others packed all of Delaney's things and brought them to their clubhouse, which worked out well because once she started working at our school system on a full-time basis, we didn't have the time we wanted to make a trip to South Carolina.

My eyes nearly bug out of my head when I hear the total, but I hand my card to clerk over Delaney's objections. "Nope, babe, not happening. If I'm with you, I pay, remember?"

"Oh, that's so chivalrous," the clerk replies, handing me my receipt along with the fifty bags full of insanity my woman bought.

"More like caveman-like," Delaney retorts, sticking her tongue out at me as she pushes the cart out to put it back where the others are at, just inside the door.

"Got a better use for that tongue, woman," I tease as I hit the button on my key fob to unlock my truck. Once I have her door open, I quickly restore feeling to my arms by dumping all the bags in the back seat, then round the truck to get into the driver's side.

Leaning over, I cup her face and kiss her, uncaring that we're in the middle of one of the busiest fucking parking lots I've ever been in. "See?" I say against her lips once I pull back.

"Mmhm," she replies, her eyes now at half-mast. "Have you told her about the dog yet?"

"No, figured we'd do that once we got there. Seems like it took him forever, but I trust Nick, and know he wanted to find the best possible match for her."

She grins while getting her seatbelt on. "Come on, Asa, time's wasting! She could already have the baby and here you are, poking along."

"I'll give you poking along, Pixie."

"So, what's her name?" Delaney asks, smiling at the sweet baby girl I'm currently holding. I'm glad we managed to get here before the baby arrived; Delaney would've never let me hear the end of it, that's for sure.

I watch my cousin smile at her man, before she turns and looks directly at me. Somehow, I know the next words out of her mouth are going to rock my world and when she says, "Natalie Asa Winters," I barely manage to keep from stepping back in shock.

Looking down at Natalie, I smile while running my finger down her silky cheek. Someday, this will be me and Delaney, but for now, I have a new little cousin to watch out for. Not like she doesn't have a club full of men ready to go to battle for her; they proved that when they took out those who hurt Honor. While I was upset we weren't called into the fray, at the end of the day, I got it.

Sometimes, you just have to handle shit and deal with the pissed off cousin who didn't get his shot. When Gunner called to tell me, he did apologize, but I understood. As long as Honor is happy and healthy, I didn't need to exact any kind of vengeance on her behalf.

"Did y'all buy the fucking store out?" Savage asks, rummaging through the countless bags I brought up once Honor was moved into a room. "Jesus, they got everything with this fucking beaver on it!"

Delaney and Honor giggle while I just shake my head. "We love the place!" Honor exclaims. "They have my favorite saltwater taffy there, Savage."

"Yeah, so pay attention," I chide. "She expects it any time you're within a twenty-mile radius of the fucking place."

"That's why we got prospects, babe. They can make runs."

"It's not the same," Honor advises, pouting. I'd believe she was actually upset if she hadn't just winked at Delaney who is now covering her mouth to keep from laughing out loud.

I shrug because if push came to shove, I'd send a prospect. Especially if I had something else that was more important to deal with besides tracking down a favorite treat. Then again, I'd go to the ends of the earth for my woman, so I suspect that while Savage may be throwing that out there, he'd do the same. I've been watching how he is with my cousin and am happy to see the dark cloud that used to hang over her is now mostly gone.

I say mostly because Delaney has told me that Honor shared she still struggles. But she's got a new job as a nurse, now has a baby to keep her further grounded, and a man and brother who would walk through the fires of Hell for her.

"Maybe not, but if you could have me home with you or running the roads while you handled the baby, which would you want?" Savage asks, pulling out another outfit and shaking his head. "Did you get one in every size or something? You act as though the store's going out of business!"

"No, I figured we'd get a few different sizes because babies tend to grow fast," Delaney retorts. "Plus, it's not like your club isn't the same as ours. Babies are always popping up like rabbits."

I hide my grin because if what I suspect is true, Delaney's going to be eating her own words at some point.

"Yeah, whatever. Are y'all hungry? I'll send a prospect out to grab some food," Savage mutters, his head *still* in the fucking bags. "Oh, here, babe, think this is for you," he says, handing her a bag of cinnamon saltwater taffy.

She squeals and eagerly rips the top off and the next thing I know, both women are unwrapping the candies and popping them into their mouths. "Okay, you two are obviously going to eat candy. What about you, Glacier? Gunner said he was going to put an order in at the local steakhouse, we can add two more."

Nodding, I say, "Yeah, that sounds good. Steaks, both cooked medium, baked potatoes, one fully loaded, one with butter and sour cream only."

"What about vegetables?" he asks, now looking at his phone. "Says they've got grilled asparagus, green beans, and some seasonal crap."

"Pixie?" I ask, turning to Delaney before bursting out into laughter. Her cheeks are so stuffed with the chewy candies she looks like a chipmunk, and she adds to it when she crosses her eyes at me. "Okay, let's go with two green beans."

I can take or leave vegetables, but for my woman's sake, I try to eat them since she says they help keep us healthy or some shit.

"Got it. Should be here in about thirty or so minutes," he advises. Looking at me, he asks, "Did your woman buy out every baby store by y'all?"

Laughing, I shrug. "She said she was taking her role as the fun auntie seriously. Except, if Honor and I are cousins, then she's really going to be the fun cousin, I guess. Fuck, I don't know."

"We also wanted to ask if you both would be her godparents," Savage remarks.

"You want us to be her godparents?" Delaney asks, looking shocked.

"Yes, we do," Honor replies, nodding.

"I'm honored," I whisper, looking down at the little girl who's already stolen a piece of my heart. "I'll always be there when you need me, little one. No matter what."

———⚜———

While Natalie sleeps, we finish off the best steak dinner I've had in a while, Delaney and Honor sitting on her bed while Savage and I sit in chairs alongside them. "Now that we're full, I wanted to say something," I tell

Honor. "Several months back, Atlas reached out to the guy who got Koba and Ridley for him and Patsy. They looked into it and found that there are some dogs who can be trained to tell when a diabetic's scent changes so that they can test themselves before they end up in a crisis situation. He reached out to Nick from the Black Tuxedos MC to see if he could help. He also asked Nick if it was possible that the dog be trained as a guard dog, since he knew from Patsy how valuable one would be to your overall peace of mind."

"What did he find out?" Honor asks. I can see hope shining in her eyes and smile.

"He's got two for you to meet as soon as you're able to travel to Texas. If you want, we'll come too so we can help Savage with Natalie while you're training with Nick. He takes a hands-on approach, and makes sure you and the dog are a good match before he lets you go home, so you don't have to worry about being given a dog then sent on your way."

"That might help," she says, looking over at Savage. To us she states, "There are good and bad days. Mostly good, but sometimes, the fear is overwhelming. It's been causing my numbers to fluctuate a lot more than I'd like, to be honest, and I'm sure Savage would feel better knowing I had a dog who could handle any threat to me or the baby."

"Yeah, it would," he finally says, squeezing Honor's hand. "Especially now that the baby's here. Gotta be able to have my head in whatever Hammer needs me doing, and knowing you'll have a dog by your side that'll take down any potential threat eases my mind."

"Then we'll get it set up," I reply. "Now, we're off to the hotel so y'all can bond together as a family of three," I say, reaching my hand out to help Delaney off the bed. "Call or text if there's anything you need us to pick up for you. Glad Gunner had the prospects grab all the bags."

Savage chuckles. "Yeah, and they better not fuck with anything in them, or they'll never get their patch."

"I'm sure Avery or Zinnia is already working on washing all the clothes and blankets," Honor replies. "Thank you both for being here. It means the world to me, to us."

"Wouldn't have missed it for the world, squirt."

"Don't call me squirt!"

EPILOGUE

Delaney

"I can't believe how much she's already grown!" I exclaim, looking down at Natalie.

"Well, she *is* two months old," Honor retorts, rolling her eyes at me.

"Glad we were finally able to get here," Savage says, looking around at the cabin where Nick set us up. "Fucking long-ass trip, that's for sure, especially with a baby in tow."

"At least you trailered your bike like I did," Glacier points out. "Nick said we were welcome to ride with his brothers later if we wanted."

"Yeah, I need some wind therapy."

Honor snickers and I look at her to see her mouthing that she'll tell me when they leave.

"Well, let's let you guys go do your manly biker thing, then," I sass, leaning up to kiss Asa. I try to call him Glacier when we're around everyone at home, but since the other ol' ladies use their men's' names interchangeably, I do as well. I'm sure there are other clubs out there who would see it as disrespectful, but thankfully, Asa says they don't feel that way.

"When will I meet the dogs?" Honor asks.

"Nick said he'd be back shortly to take us all over to The Sanctuary for you to meet them," Asa replies. "Then, once the dog's chosen you, we'll come back here while y'all train for a bit. After that, we'll go for a ride before we grab some dinner. How's that?"

"Sounds like a well-thought-out plan," I tease, earning me a swat on my ass. "Hey now, no hitting that or you won't be hitting that later."

"Mmhm, like you can resist me," he says, smirking at me.

"Are you going to tell her?" he asks me as we get ready for the day. It's been a little over a week in Texas and while Honor trains with Mackie, the dog who chose her, we hang out with Savage and Natalie, seeing the local sights.

"What do you think?" I reply, applying my mascara. "Of course, I am! I just can't believe the damn implant failed!"

It's the same thing I've been saying for over a month now because I'm still kind of in shock. Then, because I had a few scares early on, we decided to wait until I was past the danger zone. Now safely in the second trimester, with a tiny baby bump that's made its presence known, it's time to start sharing the news with my family.

"I don't remember much about that kind of shit, but do seem to recall reading the paperwork and seeing that most birth control is rendered ineffective if antibiotics are ingested."

"Damn, you almost sound like you memorized the paper or something!" I exclaim, giggling. "Yeah, who knew a simple sinus infection could cause it to fail. Good thing the doctor insisted on a pregnancy test before she implanted the new one, huh?"

Glacier

I nod, even though I suspected she was pregnant long before she went to get her new implant inserted. She had all the signs I remembered from the other ol' ladies in the club; incessant cravings, periods of weepiness and moodiness, and she was beyond horny.

"Just know that before he or she arrives, my ring's gonna be on your finger, Pixie," I tell her.

"Ah, so you just wanna marry me because I'm pregnant?" she asks.

Realizing rather quickly I'm in imminent danger depending on how I respond, I slowly shake my head. "No, ma'am. I've had this for a few months now, long before I knew there was a possibility you could be pregnant," I say, pulling the ring out of my pocket where it's been steadily burning a hole.

"Asa?" Her voice now sounds shaky as I drop to my knee in front of her and take her hand in mine.

"Delaney, when you barged into my life, my only focus was finding Honor. Then when I realized everything she'd told me about you was true, I fought hard against my attraction, using my past to shield me from the possibility of a future with you. You broke through my walls anyhow, rescuing me from becoming a bitter man. You're already my ol' lady, but will you do me the honor of being my wife?" I ask.

"Yes, yes, a thousand times yes," she shrieks, jumping into my arms. "God, I love you so much, Asa! I couldn't ask for a better man to be by my side as we walk this journey called life together."

"I love you too, Pixie. Now, as much as I want to celebrate, we're supposed to meet them for breakfast before they head back home, remember? We've gotta get on the road as well, I've got helmets to paint."

She giggles before giving me one last kiss. "Yeah, I know. Just know when we stop for the night, I'm collecting."

"Wouldn't have it any other way."

I'm pretty sure I can be classified as hearing impaired at this point seeing as Honor shrieked when she saw Delaney's ring. They've spent the past thirty minutes talking about weddings, dresses, and a bunch of other shit I have no interest in. As long as Poseidon's willing to officiate, we can have it in the middle of the fucking clubhouse for all I care.

"You know damn well you're going to give her whatever she wants," Savage whispers to me. Not like either of the women is paying us a lick of attention.

"You're right, but why all the huge drama and shit? Get someone to say the words then have a party," I retort.

"It's something they all dream about from the time they're old enough to cogitate," he states. When I give him a look he shrugs. "Hey now, I know big words."

I tune back into the women's conversation when I hear Honor gasp. "Wait, you're what? Pregnant?"

Delaney's blushing but her smile is radiant as she nods. "Yeah, we've known for about a month, but after a few scares, we decided to wait to tell anyone until the danger was past," she replies. "Y'all are the first who know outside of us and the doctor."

Honor looks at me then at Savage before she claps her hands and starts laughing almost hysterically. "You know what this means don't you?" she asks Savage, almost bouncing in her seat.

"What?"

"We have to stop at Buc-ee's!" she exclaims.

"Fuccck," we both reply in unison, with Delaney now joining in on Honor's laughter.

"Payback's a bitch, man," Savage teases, punching me in the arm.

I look at the other adults sitting around me, little Natalie cuddled in my arms. Leaning down I whisper, "Don't worry, they're not always this crazy, sweet girl."

"Yeah, sometimes, we're crazier."

Later that night, in a hotel somewhere along I-20, I show Delaney how much she means to me, whispering words into her ear as we both find our release. "Thank you for rescuing me, babe. I didn't realize I was damaged by my past until you broke through those walls."

"We rescued each other, Asa. Just like Savage rescued Honor. It's what we do for those we love," she replies, her voice sounding sleepy.

Curling her into me, I kiss her temple. "Get some rest, babe. We've got about five or six more hours to go tomorrow depending on traffic."

"Can't wait to be home."

Home.

It's always going to be where she's at, whether that's in a hotel off a busy interstate or in our cottage home by the coast.

THE END...
(NICK'S STORY CAN BE FOUND IN THE BLACK TUXEDOS MC SERIES; HE'S BOOK TWO)

ABOUT THE AUTHOR

I am a transplanted Yankee, moving from upstate New York when I was a teenager. I'm a mom of four and grandma of nine who has found a love of traveling that I never knew existed! I live with the brat-cat pack (all rescues) as well as my dog, Bosco, 'deep in the heart of Texas', as I plot and plan who will get to "talk" next!

Find me on Facebook!
https://www.facebook.com/darlenetallmanauthor
Darlene's Dolls (my reader's group):
https://www.facebook.com/groups/1024089434417791/ permalink/1063976267095774/?comment_id= 1063979757095425&notif_id=1539553456785632&notif_t= group_comment

DARLENE'S BOOKS

The Black Tuxedos MC

1. Reese - The Black Tuxedos MC
2. Nick - The Black Tuxedos MC
3. Matt - The Black Tuxedos MC

Poseidon's Warriors MC

1. Poseidon's Lady
2. Trident's Queen
3. Loki's Angel
4. Brooks' Bride
5. Atlas' World
6. The Warriors' Hearts (novella)
7. Kaya's King
8. Chelsea's Knight

DARLENE'S BOOKS

9. Orion's Universe
10. Glacier's Thaw - releasing 10/7/23

Zephyr Hills Phantoms MC (Mayhem Makers)

1. The Enforcer
2. The SAA (releases 10/15/23)

Writing in the Rogue Enforcers World

Paxton: A Rogue Enforcers Novel
Esmerelda: A Rogue Enforcers Novel
Charisma: A Rogue Enforcers Novella (with Liberty Parker)

Writing in the Royal Bastards MC world (Roanoke, VA chapter)

1. Brick's House
2. A Very Merry Brick-mas
3. Banshee's Lament
4. Jingles' Belle - releasing 12/23

Standalones

Bountiful Harvest
His Firefly
His Christmas Pixie

Her Kinsman-Redeemer
Operation Valentine
His Forever
Forgiveness
Christmas With Dixie
Our Last First Kiss
Draegon: The Falder Clan - Book One
Scars of the Soul
Hale's Song
Mountain Ink: Mountain Mermaids Sapphire Lake
Knox's Jewel: A Dark Leopards MC Novella
Desire: A Savage Wilde Novel
Contraryed: A Heels, Rhymes & Nursery Crimes short story
Sashy's Salvation
Search & Find
Little Red's
What I Like About Sunday
Starting Over With You

Rebel Guardians MC (with Liberty Parker)

1. Braxton
2. Hatchet
3. Chief
4. Smokey & Bandit
5. Law
6. Capone

DARLENE'S BOOKS

7. A Twisted Kind of Love

Rebel Guardians Next Generation (with Liberty Parker)

1. Talon & Claree
2. Jaxson & Ralynn
3. Maxum & Lily

New Beginnings (with Liberty Parker)

1. Reclaiming Maysen
2. Reviving Luca
3. Restoring Tig

Where Are They Now? RGMC updates on original 7 couples (with Liberty Parker)

1. Braxton
2. Hatchet
3. Chief

Nelson Brothers (with Liberty Parker)

1. Seeking Our Revenge
2. Seeking Our Forever
3. Seeking Our Destiny

DARLENE'S BOOKS

Rebellious Christmas (A Christmas Novella) (with Liberty Parker)

Nelson Brothers Ghost Team Series (with Liberty Parker)

1. Alpha
2. Bravo

Old Ladies Club (with Kayce Kyle, Erin Osborne and Liberty Parker)

1. Old Ladies Club - Wild Kings MC
2. The Old Ladies Club - Soul Shifterz MC
3. Old Ladies Club - Rebel Guardians MC
4. Old Ladies Club - Rage Ryders MC

The Mischief Kitties (with Cherry Shephard)

The Mischief Kitties in Bampires & Ghosts & New Friends, Oh My!
The Mischief Kitties in the Great Glitter Caper
The Mischief Kitties in You Can't Takes Our Chicken

Raven Hills Coven (with Liberty Parker)

1. Rise of the Raven
2. Whimsical

3. Enchantment
4. Prophecy Revealed

Tattered and Torn MC (with Erin Osborne)

1. Letters from Home/War (novella)
2. Letters Between Us (novella)
3. Letters of Healing (novella)
4. Letters from Mom (novella)
5. Letters to Heaven (novella)
6. Letters with Love (novella)
7. Letters from Nanny (novella)
8. Letters of Wisdom (novella)
9. Band of Letters - all 8 novellas in one volume
10. Her Keeper
11. Her One
12. Her Absolution

Printed in Great Britain
by Amazon